"WHY DON'T YOU COME OVER TO THE PATROL CAR?" HE SUGGESTED QUIETLY.

"Officer, this is ridiculous! I can explain everything."

He turned and walked to the car, leaving Laurette no choice but to follow.

"Now then, what's your name?" He spoke with an official briskness.

"Laurette Haily." She hurried on. "You see, I came here to get a cold soda and I put my money in the machine and didn't get anything so I—" He had turned on the dome light and now she could see his face clearly. He was smiling, and there was something very familiar about that smile.

"Hello, Etty," he said softly.

She tilted her head to one side and studied the policeman. He was a handsome man with brown eyes and hair, a straight nose, and a square jaw. He looked a lot like the boy she'd had a crush on all through high school. "Jeff?" she said doubtfully.

His smile deepened. "In the flesh."

A CANDLELIGHT ECSTASY SUPREME

STEAL AWAY

Candice Adams

A CANDLELIGHT ECSTASY SUPREME

Published by
Dell Publishing Co., Inc.
1 Dag Hammarskjold Plaza
New York, New York 10017

ISBN: 0-440-17861-4

Printed in the United States of America

First printing—August 1984

For Neff Rotter, with appreciation

To Our Readers:

Candlelight Ecstasy is delighted to announce the start of a brand-new series—Ecstasy Supremes! Now you can enjoy a romance series unlike all the others—longer and more exciting, filled with more passion, adventure, and intrigue—the stories you've been waiting for.

In months to come we look forward to presenting books by many of your favorite authors and the very finest work from new authors of romantic fiction as well. As always, we are striving to present the unique, absorbing love stories that you enjoy most—the very best love has to offer.

Breathtaking and unforgettable, Ecstasy Supremes will follow in the great romantic tradition you've come to expect *only* from Candlelight Ecstasy.

Your suggestions and comments are always welcome. Please let us hear from you.

Sincerely,

The Editors
Candlelight Romances
1 Dag Hammarskjold Plaza
New York, New York 10017

CHAPTER ONE

Laurette looked out the kitchen window at the Tennessee hills and smiled to herself. It was good to be here. After the last few months in Sunnyvale, California, the backwoods promised serenity and a summer without pressure. Of course, any place far away from the mad pace of Silicon Valley would probably have looked peaceful. More importantly, backwoods Tennessee offered a refuge from painful reminders of her failed marriage.

" 'Cuse me, Etty." Her grandfather reached around her to retrieve several glass canning jars from the counter. "I've got to wash a few of these."

She scooted out of his way and looked fondly at the thin old man with a shock of white hair. "I'll dry. What are you using them for?" she asked curiously.

"Things." He busied himself at his task.

Laurette didn't press the point. Grandfather had been eager and excited when she had told him she'd like to spend the summer with him. Yet, since her arrival this morning, he had seemed guarded, almost secretive. All those years of living alone had made him a very private person, Laurette decided. She would have to be careful not to intrude upon that privacy.

As Laurette dried the jars, she covertly studied her grandfather. He still stood ramrod straight, although he was thinner than he had once been and his hair was pure white, having long since lost all vestiges of its original red. He wore his clothes baggy and shuffled around in house slippers two sizes too large for him. He looked like a fragile, gentle old man. Of course, anyone who'd seen him at his most cantankerous knew better.

He began slowly to gather up the jars. "I guess I'll take these out to the shed."

"I'll help," she offered.

"No. You'd get your clean clothes dirty out there."

Laurette didn't argue. She merely held the door and then watched him heading toward the old white-washed shed. It, the aging smokehouse, and a small barn were all that remained of what had once been an eighty-acre farm. Now nearly all of the land Grandfather had once farmed had been sold and developed. Newer houses surrounded the old clapboard farmhouse and the town of Locust Grove had expanded to include Grandfather's property—to his everlasting dismay. He positively hated being within the city limits.

As he disappeared into the shed she let the back door swing closed and went upstairs to finish unpacking. As she put her clothes in the cedar-lined closet she was careful to duck at the side of the room where the roof sloped in. Working slowly, she

12

hummed to herself, pausing now and then to peek out the dormer window at the overgrown garden. Beyond it loomed the Smokies, beautifully colored in shades of blue and purple. Layers of mist were tucked between the tree-covered mountains like ponds of fog.

It had been twelve years since Laurette had spent more than a few days in Locust Grove, but she had thought of it frequently during those last months in California. The little town in eastern Tennessee had seemed an idyllic retreat, far removed from her high-pressure job as a computer designer. More importantly, Tennessee held the lure of comfortable familiarity that she had longed for during the break-up of her marriage. It had been six months since her divorce, and the scars were slowly beginning to heal. But what was she going to do with her life now?

Like Scarlett O'Hara, she decided she wouldn't think about the future now. Instead, she emptied the last suitcase and hung her clothes in the closet before going downstairs to join Grandfather in front of the television. By the time darkness fell he was fast asleep in his chair, snoring with more vigor than rhythm. Smiling tenderly, Laurette covered him with a flannel blanket, turned off the set, and wandered out into the kitchen, a vintage 1920's room complete with oak cabinets with glass doors and a white marble counter top.

Idly she took a glass from the cabinet and began searching for a cola. It would be nice to sit on the front porch swing with a cold drink in her hand. When she couldn't find any cola she decided it'd be just as nice to go for a stroll, stopping by the gas station to buy a can of soda from the vending machine.

Laurette picked up her purse and started toward the front door, pausing on the way out for a quick look into the antique beveled mirror near the door. Her short honey-colored hair was brushed away from her face, revealing a perfect oval accented with green eyes and a smattering of freckles across her nose. She had never decided if it was the freckles or the ski-slope nose that made her look younger than her twenty-nine years. But she had long since resigned herself to the fact that she would never have the kind of sultry and mysterious face she had so longed for as a teenager.

"*C'est la vie,*" she murmured, and left, noiselessly closing the door. Outside, crickets hummed and nightbirds chirped. From one of the houses came the sound of a stereo playing and a baby crying. It had been a long time since she'd had the luxury of listening to the sounds of summer in a small town. In fact, it had been a long time since she'd focused on anything except her troubled marriage to Stan and her growing unhappiness at her job with Techcorp Computers.

Laurette took her time walking to the gas station, swinging her purse absently as she passed the rows of neat bungalows and the occasional modern split-level house. The neighborhood hadn't changed much since the days when she and her gang of girls and boys had played on its streets. Their innocent games and laughter had gradually given way to adolescent preoccupations, with the boys becoming worldly and disdainful of childhood games while the girls were suddenly busy combing their hair and stealing glances at the boys. The summer she had turned seventeen her family had moved to Missouri and she had not seen her childhood companions since. What had happened to them since that summer, and what were they like now? she wondered.

She was so engrossed in her thoughts that she almost had walked past the service station before she realized it. She found the vending machines in a dark corner on the north side. Two cola machines stood side by side and she inserted two quarters into the slot of one, made her selection, and waited. Nothing happened. She pushed the button again. Still nothing happened.

Impatient, she knocked on the side of it. Further banging and jostling of the coin return produced no results. And, oddly, she was now desperate for the cola that she had been only mildly interested in before. If she'd thought of bringing more quarters, she could have tried the other machine.

But her pride balked at the thought of dropping more money into the slot. Feeling wronged and indignant, she slammed her hand hard against the machine. The palm of her hand hit the metal lock and her hand began to throb.

She was not going to take this lying down! She was going to complain to the station owner tomorrow. She was going to write to the manufacturer of the vending machine and to her congressman. She was going to . . . Blinking, Laurette peered closer at the padlock. Now that her eyes had become accustomed to the dim light she could see that the lock wasn't completely closed.

There was some justice in the world after all, she decided smugly. With one brisk movement she pulled the lock off and swung the door open and reached into the change bin for her money.

"Just what the hell do you think you're doing?"

Laurette froze, a handful of quarters clenched in her fist. There was something ominous and unyielding about the tone of that voice. And it occurred to her that her actions weren't going to be easy to explain. Hesitantly she turned away from the machine and stared at the man standing near her. The light was behind him, leaving his face in shadows beneath a flat-brimmed hat, but she could see that his shoulders were broad and his thighs trim but muscular. Then she saw the gun on his hip and the stripes down his sides. He was a policeman. Just her luck, she reflected sadly.

"What's going on here?" he demanded.

Laurette drew a deep breath and began. "I lost fifty cents in this machine and I was getting it back." It was amazing how guilty she felt, considering that she hadn't done anything wrong. Even her voice sounded too high-pitched and unconvincing.

The officer folded his arms across his chest and stood with his legs spread. "You broke the lock on the machine to retrieve fifty cents?"

"I didn't break the lock! The bolt wasn't fastened. I simply opened the machine and—" She unclenched her hands and spread them open in a gesture of innocence. Unfortunately, when she did, several quarters fell to the ground. Both she and the policeman stared down at the rolling coins. Her spirits drooped and she groped for words.

"Why don't you come over to the patrol car?" he suggested quietly.

"Officer, this is ridiculous! I can explain everything."

He turned and walked to the car, leaving Laurette no choice but to follow. She slid in on the passenger's side, where she laced her fingers together and tried to calm herself. Once she explained the situation rationally, he would realize this was all a simple misunderstanding.

"Now then, what's your name?" He spoke with an official briskness that suggested his next step would be to read her her rights and book her.

"Laurette Haily." She hurried on. "You see, I came here to get a cold soda and I put my money in the machine and didn't get anything so I—" She broke off abruptly. He had turned on the dome light and now she could see his face clearly. He was smiling and there was something very familiar about that smile.

"Hello, Etty," he said softly.

She tilted her head to one side and studied the policeman. He was a handsome man with brown eyes and hair and a straight nose and square jaw. He looked a lot like the boy she'd had a crush on all through high school. "Jeff?" she said doubtfully.

His smile deepened. "In the flesh."

In the twelve years since she'd seen him last he'd

17

grown taller, developed muscles, and become a man, and an appealing one at that. Her surprise gave way to delight and she impetuously threw her arms around his neck. "I can't believe it! It's so good to see you!" Beaming happily, she leaned back to study him more fully.

"It's good to see you too, Etty." His eyes moved over her approvingly. "You look great."

"Thanks." She shook her head to clear it, and withdrew her arms from around his neck. It was hard to believe this broad-shouldered man was the same person as the boy who had teased her about her lisp when she was five, taught her to swing a bat when she was nine, and inspired a severe crush when she was twelve. In fact, she'd been smitten with him all through high school although he never seemed to notice. She looked at his uniform and laughed. "I never thought *you'd* become a policeman."

"I never thought you'd be reduced to robbing vending machines," he countered with lazy humor.

"I didn't! That idiotic machine swallowed my money without delivering a cola and I was just getting the money back." She would have said more, but his chuckle stopped her.

"I believe you. You've got an honest face. Always have had," he added, and reached out to touch her cheek.

It was a brief touch, but in that instant when his palm rested against her cheek she experienced more than the warmth of his hand. She felt an erotic current that had nothing to do with childhood friendship pass between them. And she recognized that Jeff had felt it too.

"Let me close things up here and I'll take you somewhere to get that cold drink you came after." He got out of the car.

As he picked up the scattered quarters and locked the machine her eyes lingered on him. Jeff had definitely grown into a good looking man. He moved with the fluid masculine grace of a man whose muscles are in perfect tone. A moment later he slid back into the driver's seat and pulled out of the gas station.

"How long are you going to be in town?" he asked in a conversational tone.

"A couple of months," she said vaguely. The future, with all its uncertainties, was something she wasn't ready to face. Not yet. When she had walked out of Techcorp for good two days ago she had felt only a sense of relief to escape a world where everyone seemed absorbed in their work to the point of obsession. The twelve-hour days and seven-day weeks were over. Finally her life was going to be her own again. But what was she going to do with it?

She had the whole summer to answer that question, Laurette told herself resolutely, and turned to look out the car window as Jeff drove down Main street. Some of it had changed, she noted, and some had remained the same. The video arcade was new, but the soda fountain dated back to the early 1950's. The furniture store had a new façade, but was still owned by the Rileys. The wrought iron gas lamps from the late 1890's still dotted the street.

"Here we are." Jeff pulled into an alley and parked the car.

Laurette shot him a puzzled look. "But this is the police station."

"I know. It's eleven o'clock and all the restaurants and stores are closed. We keep cold drinks here," he explained before opening her car door and ushering her in the back door of the station.

Inside, she looked around at the green metal filing cabinets, wooden desks, and door that must lead back to the jail cells. The large room wasn't exactly homey, but it looked functional. Jeff strode across to a refrigerator in the corner and pulled out two cans of soda. He flipped the lids off each and handed one to her.

"Have a seat, Etty."

She sat down in front of his desk while he eased himself into a swivel chair behind it and leaned back. Taking off his hat, he pitched it onto the center of the desk and began running his fingers through his thick brown hair.

Laurette sipped her drink and deliberately tried not to stare at Jeff. But it was difficult to keep from doing so. She wanted to take a good look at this person she had once known so well. Where did her teenage friend leave off and the man who was a stranger begin? His voice was certainly deeper now. It had a Tennessee cadence she found very pleasant. And he sat quietly, no longer the fidgety boy eager to be off running through fields and swimming in the creek.

"I guess you and I have some catching up to do,"

he said with a slow smile. "What have you been doing with yourself for the past twelve years?"

"I went to Stanford. After graduation I got a job in Sunnyvale, California, in the computer industry. That's where I've been ever since." She smiled faintly and added, "Well, until the day before yesterday."

He raised his eyebrows. "You quit?"

She nodded and took another sip of cola.

"Hmmm." Jeff threaded his fingers together over his flat stomach. "I heard you were married." His dark eyes watched her closely.

"I was, but I'm divorced now." Laurette left it at that. "Are you married or anything?"

"No, I'm not married." A spark of devilish amusement glinted in his eyes. "But I'm open to suggestions concerning 'anything.'"

"You got over your shyness with girls, I see," she observed with a smile, but she couldn't deny feeling a thrill of pleasure at the hint of sensuality in his words. Or perhaps it was the way he reclined, the lean coil of his body looking masculinely at ease, or the half smile hovering on his lips that caused the sensation. The years since she had last seen him had been very kind to Jeff Murray.

"I don't remember ever being shy with you," he said.

"Oh, you weren't with me," she agreed. "To you I was always 'one of the guys.'" A fact that had been to her everlasting dismay when she was in high school. "It was with girls who, ahem, 'matured' early that you used to get so tongue-tied. I can still remember your tripping all over your words with Mary Jane

21

Riley." She had been ripe, busty girl at the time Laurette's mother was hooting over her insistence that she needed a bra. "Whatever happened to Mary Jane?"

He shrugged. "She married some guy from Kentucky and moved away. Let's go back to talking about you. Do you have another job lined up?"

She smiled ruefully. "I'm afraid not. I'm not even sure what kind of work I want to do, but I'm burned out on computers. I thought I'd take some time off before I plunge back into the job market." Just then Laurette caught sight of the wall clock behind him and shot out of the chair. "It's almost midnight! I've got to get back. Grandfather would be worried to death if he woke up and found me gone."

Jeff reluctantly unfolded himself from his comfortable position and picked up his hat. On the way back to her grandfather's house they talked easily about old friends. When he stopped in front of the house, he leaned forward and gave her a gentle kiss on the lips. "That's because you're an old friend and I'm glad to see you."

But his smile was very warm and the look in his brown eyes suggested a masculine interest that reached beyond friendship.

She was still tracing her index finger around her lips as she crept noiselessly up to her room. Jeff was an attractive man. With those velvet brown eyes, easy smile, and well-toned body, he had surely enticed more than one woman. He had certainly enticed her in the past.

* * *

22

Jeff finished his last pushup and rolled over to lie on his back on the hardwood floor. He had vowed when he left the Memphis police department that he wouldn't become soft and out of shape. While Locust Grove might not be a large town, he still intended to give it superior police protection.

He toweled off the sweat from his face and chest and began to do situps. ". . . eight, nine, ten." He sank back onto the floor, breathing deeply. His leg hurt slightly and he would probably limp tomorrow.

Even after the bullet had fractured a bone in his leg, he could have stayed on with the Memphis police force. In fact, his friends there had thought he was crazy to leave, insisting he was too dedicated and energetic to be content running the police department in a small town. But he'd been in Locust Grove eight months now and he had no desire to leave. Until he'd arrived, the town had been run by an aging and easygoing police chief. Teenagers had run drag races down Main Street; burglaries had gone unsolved, and the few murders there had been were invariably reported as "apparent suicides." He had cleaned things up immediately.

Jeff grinned at his own lack of modesty—and lack of truth. He hadn't exactly succeeded in wiping out *all* crime. He was well aware that the teenagers now sneaked out to deserted country roads to pit their cars and racing ability against one another. Nor had he solved every break-in. Fortunately there had been no murders to contend with since he'd taken the job. No, he hadn't cleaned up everything, but things were definitely better. And once he got the computerized crime retrieval system working, they'd improve even more.

Rising, he sauntered into the bathroom and stripped off his gym shorts. Then he stepped into the shower and began lathering soap over himself.

Running into Laurette tonight had been a very pleasant surprise. The skinny, freckled kid he'd known had grown into a voluptuous woman with an all-American kind of beauty. He ducked his head beneath the shower and added shampoo, smiling as he recalled the sound of Laurette's laughter. It had been light and breezy, yet somehow provocative. He'd liked it. But what he'd found most compelling were her eyes. They were a shade of green almost as dark as malachite, and when she looked at him he'd felt very important. Just thinking about the way she'd looked at him made him decide to increase his number of pushups and get a haircut tomorrow.

By the time Laurette awoke the next morning, the sun was fully up and she could hear her grandfather in the kitchen below. Stretching languidly, she looked around at the green print wallpaper and the white chintz curtains. She had stayed in this room often as a child, making the then impressive journey from her parents' house three blocks away to spend the night with Grandfather. Once her family had moved to Missouri, however, they had rarely visited Locust Grove and had seldom stayed for long.

Outside the closed bedroom door she heard her grandfather trudging up the steps. He stopped outside her door and rapped. "Breakfast is ready, Etty."

She flung back the covers and pulled a robe over her nightgown. "You didn't have to make breakfast," she told him, tying the robe around her as she followed him down the stairs and into the kitchen. "I could have fixed something when I got up."

Ignoring her protest, he pointed toward a chair at the round oak table. "Jowl bacon and fresh brown eggs. Eat."

Obediently she applied herself to the food while he began washing mason jars at the sink. "Do you know what time the library opens?" she asked as she reached for a slice of bread.

"Nope."

"I guess I'll have to call and find out."

"Can't." He immersed more jars into the soapy water. "Phone was taken out last week."

Laurette stared at him in astonishment, her food forgotten. "Grandfather, *why?* You need a phone. You might need to call someone for help. Or you might get snowed in in the winter and need groceries delivered."

He snorted. "You think anyone delivers groceries nowadays? Besides, I didn't ask to have it taken out. They just came and took it," he grumbled, then drew himself up proudly. "I don't care. The whole damn company is run by a bunch of rapscallions and I'm not going to have any more dealings with them," he concluded.

"Oh, dear," Laurette murmured. When Grandfather got stubborn, nothing budged him. But she was well aware that he was too old to live without a phone.

"There's lots more eggs over here in the pan if you want them." He bent over his work again.

"I don't want any more, thanks." Laurette rose and carried her plate to the sink, pondering how she could delicately repair her grandfather's breach with the phone company. "I'll finish the dishes." Her eyes wandered over the dozens of canning jars on the marble counter top. Was Grandfather going senile? she wondered. Why else was he washing all these jars? No one had done any canning since her grandmother had died years ago. And what about the phone? Surely he had forgotten to pay his bill or something. The phone company didn't yank out a telephone without good reason.

He moved away from the sink so she could begin washing. "When you get these done there are some more jars in the basement you can wash."

She stared at him. "How many do you need?"

"As many as you can find." He shuffled toward the back door, his oversize houseshoes flapping as he walked. "Quit when you get tired."

Laurette looked over the sea of mason jars. They were of every size and description, ranging from old blue ones to brand-new jars. There were quarts and pints and half pints. She couldn't see a reason in the world to wash them, but she did anyway. When she finished the ones on the counter she went down into the basement and brought up more. If it would make Grandfather happy, then what harm could it do? Besides, it was a lazy June morning and she had nothing pressing to do.

From the kitchen window she could see the forested mountains enveloped in haze. This was Tennessee the way she always remembered it—verdant and peaceful. Being here gave her a mellow sense of well-being that lasted throughout the rest of the day and until noon the following day. That was when she went to the shed to call her grandfather to lunch. He wasn't there, but when she stepped into the dusky shed, she discovered something else—a collection of copper wash kettles, coiled tubing, and sacks of corn mash and sugar. Her grandfather was running a still!

CHAPTER TWO

Laurette stood gaping down at the collection of paraphernalia and at the filled canning jars along one wall of the shed.

"Laurette," someone called. "Where are you?"

She gasped in dismay. That was not her grandfather's voice. It was Jeff's! Frantically she looked around the crowded shed. What should she do? While Jeff was surely here for a friendly visit, he was still a police officer. If he saw the still, her grandfather would be in very big trouble.

"Laurette."

He was right outside the door. Forcing back her panic, she ran her agitated hands over her turquoise top and down to her jeans, breathed deeply, and stepped out, quickly slamming the door behind her. "Jeff, hello!" She was sunny and pleasant and moving as quickly as possible away from the shed. "Come on into the house and have a glass of iced tea," she threw over her shoulder.

"Well, I suppose I could—"

She was halfway up the back steps and Jeff was right behind her when she remembered the kitchen was full of canning jars. She froze on the top step. While she had not guessed their true purpose, Jeff might not be so naive. Smiling brilliantly, she turned back to him. "On second thought, it's lunchtime, so why don't you take me out for something to eat?"

He studied her curiously. "What about your grandfather?"

"What about him?" she breathed. Did Jeff already know about the still? Had he come to arrest her grandfather?

"What will he do for lunch?" he clarified.

She almost sagged with relief. "Oh, he likes to make his own," she said airily.

His lips moved into a winsome smile. "Good. I like the idea of having you to myself." He stepped off the bottom stair back into the yard. "Mmmm, you smell good."

"Soapsuds," she replied, hoping that was what he smelled. Or maybe he was smelling the fumes from the shed? Briskly she moved toward the front of the house. "I see you're off duty." He looked ruggedly handsome in a pair of jeans that showed the outlines of his powerful legs and a green plaid shirt that was open at the neck.

"Sort of. I've been down at the office doing a little work on my own. That's something I wanted to talk to you about. I tried to call you, but the operator said the phone had been disconnected."

"Yes, there's been a slight misunderstanding I have to get cleared up." She changed the subject. "What was it you wanted to talk to me about?"

"We'll discuss it over lunch." They had reached

29

his car, a new gray sedan with its chrome and mirrors polished to a nice shine. "What would you like to eat?" he asked as he held the door for her.

"A burger would be fine," Laurette murmured absently. But her thoughts were on Grandfather and the still. As Jeff pulled away from the curb she looked back at the house. The minute she got home she was going to find Grandfather and make him understand that he had to get rid of the still. He could get into all kinds of trouble with something like this, not only with the local police, but with the federal authorities as well.

"Did you hear me?" Jeff asked.

She started guiltily and glanced up at him. "No, I'm sorry, I didn't."

"I said we could go to Drake's Diner if you like. You remember it, don't you—the restaurant in the old caboose down by the railroad tracks?"

"Of course I remember it. You mean it's still in business?" But her mind was not on food. What if she told Jeff about her problem? He would help her, wouldn't he? After all, they were old friends. That was just it, she reflected silently, they had been friends in the *past*, but Jeff was really a stranger to her now. How did she know he wouldn't double back and arrest her grandfather the moment she made her confession? As a policeman, he might view that as his sworn duty. No, she would work this out on her own and put it out of her mind until she could.

"The old diner's still going strong," he said in answer to her question.

"How's the food?"

He glanced at her sideways, merriment in his brown eyes, although he managed to keep a straight face. "Same as it used to be."

She giggled. "That bad, huh? What the heck," she declared recklessly, "it'll be like old times." Well, not quite like old times. Then, a dozen kids would go in, buy two malts, and split them. "But I want my own malt this time," she informed him loftily.

He sighed. "I should've known you were going to be an expensive date."

"And I want French fries. With lots of catsup." She glanced down at her waist and decided to skip the fries. She had a slender figure, but had to fight a constant battle to maintain it.

Jeff drove by the old weathered bungalows on the north side of town, crossed the tracks, and parked in front of the diner. It was a little seedier than she had remembered, with crabgrass growing in the cracks in the sidewalk. A broken window had been replaced with cardboard.

They stepped inside and Jeff said hello to several people as they made their way to an empty booth near the grill. Moments later a gum-chewing waitress appeared, shouted their orders to the man at the grill, and smiled fetchingly at Jeff. He gave her only the mildest of smiles before turning his brown eyes on Laurette. For the second time she was struck with his quiet watchfulness. She wondered where and how he had acquired it. As a boy he'd always been the one to leap first and look later.

"You're staring at me," he told her politely. "What are you thinking?"

31

She smiled reflectively and looked down at the swirls in the Formica table. "That you've changed."

He laughed. "You've changed a little yourself, Etty."

"I guess I have." She wondered if Jeff felt the same confusion she did at trying to sort out the old comrade from the new acquaintance. Suddenly conscious of the lengthening silence between them and of his dark eyes gazing at her, she asked, "What was it you wanted to discuss with me?"

"I need your help," he said bluntly. "I scraped together enough money from the city to buy a small computer for the police department, but I need help programming it. I'm sure it's not nearly as sophisticated as the machines you're used to, but you'd be able to do more with it than anybody else we could hire." He studied his nails before adding pragmatically, "Besides, we can't afford to pay a computer programmer to come to Locust Grove. I'm not even sure we'd be able to pay you the minimum wage."

The request caught Laurette off guard and she frowned. She'd come two thousand miles to escape the draining, impersonal world of access codes and integrated circuits. On the other hand, Jeff needed her help and she didn't have any other plans for the summer. "I don't know," she began uncertainly.

"You could give it a try," he coaxed.

"Let me think about it."

"Okay." He grinned disarmingly. "But you won't get another offer like this." His smile turned impudent. "The pay's lousy; the hours are long, and you

32

won't get a word of gratitude. You'll always regret it if you pass it up."

She chuckled. "You make it sound very appealing."

The waitress arrived with their food and Laurette busied herself adding salt to her hamburger. But she couldn't help thinking that there was one thing Jeff had neglected to mention: the fact that she would be working closely with him. And she wasn't at all sure she wanted to spend much time with Jeff because she suspected he could end up affecting her more strongly than she was capable of handling right now.

To evade the issue, she introduced a neutral topic to the conversation. "So tell me, who's still around here from the old gang? I thought I'd look some of them up this summer."

"Not many left." He dipped a French fry into a dollop of catsup at the side of his plate. "Mary Linn and Darla moved away. James and Ralph live in Memphis. Only Kathy and Sarah are still here in town. Kathy married Grant Darnell and they have a couple of kids."

"I see." But she was more interested in Jeff than in Kathy at the moment. As a teenager Jeff had stirred girlish longings, but as a man he affected her even more strongly. In addition to being broad-shouldered and handsome, he had a charisma that drew her—and probably most women, she thought wryly—to him. Neutrality was temporarily forgotten as she cupped her chin in her hands and looked squarely into his rich brown eyes. "How come you never married, Jeff?"

He met her gaze steadily. "I haven't yet found the right girl. How come you didn't stay married?"

"I found the wrong guy," she returned lightly. Well, Stan hadn't been wrong for her in the beginning. When she'd first met him at Techcorp Computers, both of them had been totally immersed in their jobs. The mutual interest that had drawn them together had been their work. Gradually, however, Laurette had begun to feel that life was passing her by while she devoted all her energy and time to her job. But Stan's fascination with computers had continued to grow and he had gladly put in long hours of overtime and brought his work home with him. At first she had competed for his attention and tried to think of ways to stitch up their raveling marriage. But he had continued to slip further away, becoming more and more remote from her, until she had felt that she was living with a stranger.

Jeff glanced at his watch. "I have an appointment with someone in a few minutes. I guess I'd better take you home," he said reluctantly.

Fifteen minutes later he dropped her off at her grandfather's house. "Think about my offer." With a perfectly straight face he added, "Don't take too long or we'll hire someone else." His eyes were dark with cheeky amusement.

"I'd hate for that to happen," she murmured. "I'll let you know."

As soon as she had closed the car door and glanced at her grandfather's house, the problem of the still leapt back into her mind. She waited until Jeff drove away before going in search of her grandfather. She found him in the shed putting lids on jars brimming with amber liquid. The strong fumes of alcohol permeated the air.

Grandfather jerked his head up when she entered, then began waving his arms at her as if she were an unwanted chicken scratching around in his flower bed. "I don't want you coming in 'ere!"

Ignoring him, Laurette pulled the door closed behind her. "I know you don't want me in here and I know why. That's home brew you're making and if you don't stop this instant, you're going to end up in a lot of trouble." She felt a little odd lecturing her seventy-nine-year-old grandfather; in the past he had always been the one to do the scolding. But she stood her ground firmly.

Grandfather grumbled under his breath. "A fellow can make himself a little 'shine if he wants as long as he don't sell it to nobody else."

She pursed her lips and looked around at the scores of bottles. "In the first place, I don't think it's legal to distill alcohol under any circumstances. Besides, I can't believe *all* of this is for you."

"Most of it is. I give only a little away to friends." Under her unrelenting gaze he confessed. "Well, they pay me a bit. Just to offset expenses, you understand." Abruptly he returned to putting lids on the jars, his back a stiff line that bespoke mulishness.

Laurette spread her hands in a gesture of frustration. "Grandfather, this is *illegal*. Don't you understand what that means if you get caught?"

"I won't get caught." He reached for another lid.

35

"Oh, no? Did you know a policeman was here today?"

"A policeman!" He straightened and stared at her, then rumpled his hand through his white hair until it stood up on his head like pickets.

She nodded emphatically. "Yes, a policeman. He was right outside the door of this shed. If I hadn't managed to get him away, he probably would have found the still."

"You got him away?" His face lit up with approval. "Good girl."

She rolled her eyes upward in exasperation. "Grandfather, promise me you'll get rid of this thing."

He scratched his head morosely. "You say he was outside the shed?"

"Just outside the door." She pointed for added effect.

"Then I guess I don't have much choice," he muttered.

"No, you don't."

"Seems a shame . . ." His voice trailed off mournfully.

Laurette left him in the shed mumbling about the death of free enterprise in this country, and returned to the house. Once there, she tried to settle down with a book but couldn't concentrate. Every few moments she popped up and went to look out the back window. She saw Grandfather go to the barn and return a short time later dragging several empty burlap bags. Good. The sooner he hauled the moonshine paraphernalia to the dump, the better.

* * *

Kathy Darnell looked very much as she had when she had been a high school cheerleader. She was still blond, still bubbly, and weighed only a trifle more than when she'd done such superb splits. She greeted Laurette at the door of her modern house, hugged her, then stepped back and surveyed her with a grin.

"You were a late bloomer, but you certainly look marvelous now," Kathy declared.

"Thanks. You look good yourself."

"Come in. The kids are at Grant's mother's, so we have the place to ourselves. We can chat to our hearts' content." She led the way into the family room, with its maple furniture and gold striped sofa and chairs. "Sit here in the reclining chair. It's the most comfortable. I'll get us some coffee." She left and returned a moment later bearing a tray with coffee, cream, and sugar. "You are a sight for sore eyes. I haven't seen you in ages."

"Not since I was seventeen," Laurette agreed, and helped herself to a cup of black coffee.

They spent the next hour catching up on news about old friends.

Finally Kathy brought up Jeff's name. "Jeff Murray's still around. As I recall, you were always sweet on him. He's the police chief here," she related.

"It seems odd that he never left Locust Grove," Laurette said casually.

"Oh, he did. He was a policeman in Memphis for several years." Kathy furrowed her brow thoughtfully. "I think he was even a detective." She shrugged when the specifics eluded her. "Anyway, he got several medals in Memphis. I remember reading about him in the paper."

"Then why did he come back here?" Laurette wondered more to herself than to Kathy.

"He was injured in Memphis. He got shot in the leg or something," she said offhandedly. "He still limps sometimes."

"Oh." Laurette got a funny feeling in the pit of her stomach when she thought about Jeff being hit by a bullet.

"Besides, the town council asked him to take the job here. Mr. Peyton was ready to retire and we needed somebody with real police experience." Kathy smoothed back her blond hair and changed the subject. "How long are you going to be in town?"

"A couple of months."

"What are you going to do all summer?" Kathy asked bluntly.

Laurette smiled. "I'm not sure. Read, take walks, visit old friends." *And decide my future*, she thought.

"You're going to get bored," Kathy predicted ominously.

Laurette examined a snag on her pink terrycloth top. "If I do, then I'll help program a computer system for the police department. Jeff has asked me to."

Kathy looked at her slyly. "Oh, so you've seen him. You didn't say so."

Laurette smiled at the memory of their meeting. "We ran into each other," she said casually, electing not to mention that it had been while she was dismantling a Coke machine.

38

"He's turned into a terrific-looking man," Kathy said with frank approval. "When I see him striding about in his uniform, shoulders thrown back and hair windblown, I almost forget I'm a married woman." Her eyes drifted over Laurette. "But you aren't married." The implication could hardly have been more pointed.

"Jeff is nice-looking," Laurette agreed carefully. "But I've only been divorced a few months, Kathy. I'm not ready to get involved with any man right now." Laurette stared down at the steaming black coffee. Falling in love had been easy; falling out of love, she had discovered, was much more difficult. She had loved Stan when they got married but as he became more and more obsessed with his work she had watched helplessly as the exultant colors of their love faded.

Disillusioned and shaken by the experience, she knew one thing for certain: if she ever did fall in love again, it wouldn't be for a long time, and then she'd have to be very, very sure of what she was getting into.

The conversation turned to less personal matters. It was another full hour before Laurette finished her last cup of coffee. "I should be getting back."

Kathy rose when she did. "I'm glad you came. We'll have to get together again."

"I'd like that."

"Maybe someday we can drive over to Knoxville and visit Patsy. I know she'd be glad to see you." Kathy grinned. "Anyway, I need an excuse to go shopping. I'll call you."

Laurette shook her head. "You can't. I'm afraid we don't have a phone right now. Let me get in touch with you."

As she left Kathy's house Laurette decided that now was as good a time as any to get the problem with the phone straightened out. She walked directly to the phone company office on the edge of the downtown business district. Inside the modern building Laurette was greeted by a pleasant woman who was seated behind a desk.

"May I help you?" the secretary asked.

"I'm here concerning service on Mr. Avril Harrison's telephone."

"One moment, please."

The secretary left and returned a few moments later carrying a file folder. "Our records show that that service has been disconnected."

"Yes, I know. I'd like to have it reinstalled."

The woman sat back down behind her desk. "There's an unpaid bill that will have to be settled first."

"I'll pay the bill," Laurette assured her.

The woman looked at her doubtfully. "It's almost five hundred dollars."

Laurette blinked, then leaned forward apologetically. "I'm sorry, I don't believe I heard right. How much is the bill?"

The woman consulted the file. "Four hundred eighty three dollars and fifty-two cents."

"I—there must be some mistake."

"I'm afraid not," the secretary said patiently. "There are several overseas calls."

"Overseas," she repeated blankly. "My grandfather hasn't been out of the country since World War I. He certainly wouldn't be calling anyone outside the country."

"I'm sorry," the woman said, "but that's what our records show."

"That's just impossible. Your records must be wrong."

The woman extended the bill toward her. "Is this Mr. Harrison's number?"

Laurette looked at the phone number and address. "Well, yes, but—"

"Since these are direct-dial calls, there isn't much possibility of error. I'm afraid the customer will have to pay this bill before service can be restored," she concluded.

Clearly Laurette was getting nowhere. "May I speak with the office manager, please?"

"He's out of the office today."

"Then could you give me a copy of that bill, please?"

She left the office five minutes later armed with a copy of the bill and took it home to question Grandfather. He vehemently denied ever having made any of the long-distance calls. Her anger was fueled by his description of the high-handed manner in which his service had been disconnected. "They just goose-stepped in 'ere and yanked it out, not paying the least bit of attention to what I was trying to tell them."

"Surely there's someone who can help us," she said. Five minutes later Laurette was on her way out the door again—headed for the police station.

* * *

Jeff looked up as the door opened and Laurette sailed in. Her cheeks were flushed and her green eyes bright. She made an appealing picture even with her lustrous golden-brown hair disheveled and her words coming in a quick rush.

"I need some help. Someone has been illegally billing long-distance phone calls to Grandfather's number! I have the bill here." She waved it at him for proof. "There are fifteen calls to Europe. Europe!"

"Why don't you sit down," he suggested mildly.

Laurette paced the room, unaware that he had spoken. "My grandfather doesn't know a living soul in Rome. He can't even speak Italian! He was in Italy once," she admitted, "but that was during the war and he can't remember the name of the town he was in. It was all bombed out and—"

Jeff saw he was going to have to take matters into his own hands. Cupping a hand under her elbow, he steered her to a chair and pushed her gently down into it. "Now then, just relax a minute." He pulled a chair up next to hers and leaned forward. "Okay. Have you discussed this with the phone company?"

"I just came from there!" Her eyes flashed indignantly. "They refuse to reinstall service until the bill is paid."

Jeff pried the crumpled bill from her fingers and studied it. There were indeed a raft of overseas calls. He started to speak, then hesitated. Although he hadn't seen much of Mr. Harrison lately, he did know the old man was doing a couple of strange things. For one thing, Laurette's grandfather had

42

recently started driving twenty-three miles to the next town to shop instead of buying his food at the local stores although he hadn't had a quarrel with any of the town merchants. For another thing, Jeff had seen Mr. Harrison prowling around at the local dump. When he'd called a greeting to him, the old man had straightened as if he'd been shot and acted very stiff and odd. It was entirely possible he was going senile and simply didn't remember making the calls. Tactfully he mentioned that possibility to Laurette.

"You know, when people get older, they sometimes, ah, lose track of day-to-day events."

She drew herself up proudly. "My grandfather is not senile, if that's what you're suggesting." After a moment's pause she lowered her long, curved lashes and mumbled almost inaudibly, "I thought he might be when I first got here, but there was a reason for some actions that had seemed a little odd."

For a moment Jeff was distracted from thoughts of Laurette's grandfather. She was wearing a fuzzy pink top with spaghetti straps that revealed a delectable expanse of skin. Her darker pink divided skirt showed perfectly formed legs.

She pushed back a wisp of her short honey-colored hair and slumped in the chair. "I'm sorry, I had no business bursting in here and unloading this on you. I know it isn't a police matter, but I was just *so* mad." She clenched her hands together tightly atop her knees.

Jeff brought his wandering thoughts back to the

problem. "I think you'd be better off to go back to the phone company and talk to them again."

She nodded. "You're right, of course. I guess I just wanted to let off a little steam." She smiled weakly. "Sorry I bothered you."

"That's okay." He certainly hadn't minded. Seeing her all flushed and fiery had quickened his interest in her.

She started to rise. "I'll let you get back to work."

"Wait." Since she was here, he decided to press his cause. "Have you given any more thought to setting up a computer system for the department?" He nodded toward the small computer terminal in a corner of the room. He'd been trying to teach himself to use it by reading the instruction manual, but it was clearly going to take an expert to do any programming.

Her eyes moved to the computer, then back to him. "I hadn't made up my mind yet."

"This town needs a modernized police department," he said persuasively. "Right now I've got men doing paperwork when they should be out investigating crimes."

"You're leaning on me," she accused.

He smiled disarmingly. "I know. Does that mean you'll take the job?"

Laurette sighed dramatically. "Yes, I guess I will." She flashed that smile he was coming to like so well.

CHAPTER THREE

Behind Laurette, the front door of the station swung open and a feminine voice sang out, "Hello, Jeffrey. Busy?"

"Never too busy for you, Belinda," he responded with genial gallantry. Rising, he motioned her in. "Come here, there's someone I want you to meet."

Laurette turned then and found herself looking at a petite woman with silky black hair and an angelic face. The newcomer was wearing a peach-colored suit with a delicately ruffled white blouse. Suddenly her casual top and culottes seemed scruffy and she self-consciously whisked her fingers through her tumbled hair.

"Laurette, this is Belinda Jones. Ace reporter," Jeff added with a teasing wink at the pretty woman. "Laurette is staying here for the summer. She used to live in Locust Grove and we knew each other as kids."

"How nice." Belinda had a lovely, melodic voice.

"I'm pleased to meet you, Belinda." Laurette was annoyed to find a hoarse burr in her own voice. She cleared her throat.

Belinda transferred her attention back to Jeff. "Would it be better if I came back later to talk about the Smith burglary?"

So this was a business visit, Laurette thought. She had begun to wonder. "Don't go on my account," she said quickly as she stood up. "I've got to be leaving."

"Oh, I don't want to run you off," Belinda objected.

"No, really I have to—"

Jeff cut through the awkward exchange with a firm, "Sit down, Laurette. This will take just a minute and then we'll iron out the details of when you'll be coming to work."

"Oh, are you a police officer?" Belinda asked with new interest. As she spoke she sat down in a straight-back chair and flipped open a notebook.

"No, I'm going to be setting up the computer system for the department."

"Laurette is a computer expert. She'll be a life saver to us," Jeff affirmed as staunchly as if someone had implied otherwise. "Okay, Belinda. What is it you want to know?"

"I understand someone broke into the Smith house and stole a stereo and several other items yesterday."

Jeff pushed his fingers through his thick brown hair. "That's right."

"That area around Woods Park has been hit very heavily over the past two years. Do you think it's possible the thief is someone who lives around there?"

46

"No. The area has been heavily hit because it's the most affluent one in town," Jeff answered promptly.

He was all brisk professionalism now, and Laurette found herself watching him in fascination. The same stern man who had found her at the Coke machine was very much in evidence. There was a no-nonsense tautness to his mouth and he sat up straight, as if he had been called to attention by some invisible captain. Again she was struck by the strong lines of his chest and shoulders.

Belinda nodded and jotted on the pad. "Do you have any suspects?"

"Not yet."

The reporter's face relaxed into a smile and her eyes met his. "Will you let me have the scoop when you find out who it is?"

Jeff's voice became playfully bantering. "Of course I will, Belinda. I'll do whatever it takes to keep the other reporters at bay until I've called you."

Belinda's smile slackened into a self-mocking expression. "I suppose I must look a little ridiculous trying to do hot investigative reporting in a town where the newspaper coverage consists primarily of personal notes and pictures of the Little League team." She squared her shoulders defiantly. "But I happen to think there are other stories to be covered even in a town as small as ours."

Laurette's instinctive, unfounded sense of competition toward the attractive reporter faded and she felt a pang of sympathy. Obviously Belinda was trying hard in a job where her efforts were not always appreciated nor, Laurette suspected, her talents fully used.

"You're doing a great job at the paper," Jeff said with quiet sincerity.

Belinda brightened at the compliment and Laurette silently appreciated his sensitivity.

"Why, thank you, Jeffrey." Flipping her notebook closed, Belinda turned to Laurette. "It was nice to meet you. I'm sure we'll be running into each other again." The reporter's eyes grew softer as her gaze swung back to Jeff. "And, of course, I'll be seeing you again, Jeffrey."

Laurette watched silently. There was no mistaking Belinda's attraction to Jeff. His emotions, however, were not so easily read. He smiled broadly, even fondly, but it was hard to measure the depth of that fondness.

What difference did it make how Jeff felt about Belinda? She had come to Locust Grove to straighten out her life. It didn't matter what Jeff's relationship with Belinda might be because Laurette was not interested in him except as a friend. It was just that his eyes could sometimes look so soft and velvety and there was a charm to his smile that made her feel special and . . .

" 'Bye." With a final wave and smile, Belinda sailed out of the room.

"She seems very nice," Laurette murmured. While she meant it, she still hoped Jeff wouldn't agree too quickly.

"She is." Pushing back his chair, he rose. For a moment a pained expression flitted across his face and Laurette remembered what Kathy had told her about his leg. Before she could ask him about that, however, he was saying, "All right, when can you start work?"

"How about next week?" she suggested. The spaghetti strap of her top slipped off her shoulder. As she tugged it back into place she thought about Belinda's chic suit and immediately decided to wear something equally chic on her first day of work.

"How about starting tomorrow?" he said.

"Maybe the end of this week," she compromised.

He grinned. "How about right now?"

Laughing, Laurette reached for her purse. "Sir, I don't think you understand the first thing about bargaining."

"Teach me," he suggested, mischief lurking in his dark eyes. "I'd be a very willing student for anything you wanted to teach me, Etty."

Dangerous. Very dangerous, she warned herself as she took a step backward. The suggestive tone of his voice made her think all too clearly of satiny sheets and midnight whispers. He was intrigued by her, and she didn't want him to be. Well, yes, she did, a confused part of her argued, only she wasn't ready to respond.

Yet watching Jeff now, with his long legs slightly spread apart and his hands resting easily on his hips while his eyes held hers, her body *was* responding. A seductive warmth was curling through her, making her feel feminine and desirable and very capable of giving. *You'd better get out of here,* she warned herself. "I've got to go, Jeff."

For an instant he looked sorry, then he rebounded with a chuckle. "Be here tomorrow to start work," he commanded.

She looked directly into his dark brown eyes. "I'm not going to let you bully me, Jeff Murray. I'll be here Monday morning."

"Be sure it's bright and early Monday morning," he called after her as she started for the door.

"Slave driver!" she called back. But she really was pleased at Jeff's eagerness for her to start working with him.

Grandfather was just stepping out the front door when Laurette returned from the police station and walked up onto the porch. The third step still creaked, she noted with nostalgic approval.

"Hi!" she greeted him.

"'Lo." Her grandfather was wearing a crisp white shirt, slacks that were two sizes too big for him, and a fedora with a jaunty feather.

They met in the middle of the porch. "Where are you going?" she asked curiously.

"To the grocery story," he said gruffly.

He didn't seem to be in a particularly good mood —probably still upset over having to dismantle the still—so Laurette tactfully decided against suggesting that she join him.

"I'll be back in three hours or so."

Her eyes widened. "It takes three hours to go to the store?"

"I go to Creasons in Mountain Creek," he explained grudgingly.

"Creasons?" Puzzled, she pursued. "You mean you drive all the way over there to buy groceries? That must be twenty miles."

"Twenty-three. They have good sales." Grandfather drew himself up majestically, his eyes snapping defiantly beneath the white tufts of eyebrows.

She bit back further questions and nodded mutely. This was Grandfather's house and he was entitled to do what he wanted and go wherever he pleased. So what if Grandfather drove to another town to shop? He had little else to do with his time. "Well, have a good trip," she said pleasantly, and leaned forward to kiss his cheek.

He mumbled something and shambled off down the steps toward the old Plymouth while she went into the house. Moments later she heard the loud chugging of the 1948 Plymouth as Grandfather backed out of the driveway. She headed upstairs to her room and soon Grandfather was forgotten and her thoughts had turned to a certain man with a body that was lean with health and vitality and a face that was a bit too handsome for her own peace of mind.

Stretching out languidly on her chenille-covered bed, she closed her eyes. The more she saw Jeff, the more drawn she was to him. Which was why she was absolutely crazy to go to work at the police department. After all, she was still recovering from a divorce that had left her feeling like an empty shell in danger of caving in on itself, and she was in no state to embark on another relationship. Any sensible woman would have picked up the phone and called to tell him she wasn't going to take the job.

But she didn't feel like being sensible at the moment. Besides, she considered practically, she didn't have a phone.

That realization changed the direction of her thoughts. Should she go back to the phone company and argue with them further? But what could she say to the secretary that she hadn't said earlier. And the manager wasn't there today. With a flash of genius a better idea hit her. Why not have a new phone installed under her own name? She had good credit with the phone company and she didn't even need to mention her grandfather and his troublesome unpaid bill. Yes, that's what she'd do—she'd have a phone put in under her name and circumvent this problem of Grandfather's unpaid long-distance bills.

The matter was settled less than ten minutes later by walking next door to a neighbor and calling to request telephone service. They promised to install the phone the following day.

Jeff thought the small town summer evenings were one of the best parts of being back in Locust Grove. In Memphis he had rarely gotten out and walked, but now he went for a stroll almost every evening. He liked the fresh air and the feel of mist on his face as it wafted in from the Smokies. And it made him feel good to be greeted by name by people sitting on porch swings. He even liked the feel beneath his feet of the brick sidewalks in the older parts of town.

He felt particularly at peace tonight as he sauntered along the schoolyard and listened to the shouts of the children playing softball beneath the field lights. He had once played there himself and had taught Laurette how to catch a ball on that outfield. She'd never been great at softball, he reflected with a reminiscent smile.

Although he had known Laurette until she was seventeen he remembered her most clearly as a fresh-faced, giggly junior high girl. In high school members of the old gang had begun to go their own ways and he'd become interested in football and cars. He'd been interested in girls, too, but it had been a schoolboy's randy attraction to robust cheerleaders. His interest now was in women who were willowy and more subtly sensual—like Laurette.

Thinking about her made him decide to stroll over to her house. He felt the spring in his step as headed in that direction. Once she started working he'd be seeing a great deal of her, and he was looking forward to that. In the daytime, of course, their relationship would have to be strictly professional, but after hours—ah, that was a different matter.

He'd been thinking about Laurette often—thinking about her hair that was the perfect shade between blond and brown; about her lithe, beguiling body that had been so enticingly revealed by that pink top; about the way her lips looked softly moist and inviting when she parted them. He imagined tasting those lips and touching her bare skin.

"Stop right there, Murray," he told himself aloud and a dog nearby looked at him curiously. If he let his imagination wander any further, he'd have to go home and take a cold shower. A few moments later he walked up the creaking wooden steps of Avril Harrison's house and knocked on the door.

Laurette answered. She was dressed in a pair of green shorts and a mint green polo shirt. Her short hair was in charming disarray and she was barefoot. A smile blossomed at the sight of him.

"Well, this is a pleasant surprise," she said. Then she looked down at the uniform and her smile wilted. "Are you on duty?" she asked quickly.

"No, I just haven't changed out of my uniform."

"Who is it?" her grandfather called from the depths of his armchair.

"A friend," she called over her shoulder. In one swift movement she closed the door behind her and put her hand on Jeff's arm. "Why don't we sit out here on the swing?"

"Fine with me." Perfect, in fact. It was nice and dark out here.

Once they were seated, however, she slid away from him and looked around like a nervous sixteen-year-old.

He watched her in silence. "Is something wrong?"

"No. Nothing." She threw him a wavering smile that was just visible in the dim light coming through the window.

That was all the encouragement he needed. He moved to her side of the swing, drew her toward him, and kissed her. It was a short tentative questioning kiss, and she responded affirmatively. Their second kiss lasted a good long time. He was exploring her mouth more fully and caressing her lips, as if trying to absorb her essence into himself. The feeling of her lips and tongue pressing hungrily against his encouraged him. He gathered her closer to him and felt the softness of her body, smelled the jasmine of her perfume, and tasted the desire on her lips.

He felt a tremor run through her and heard her sigh. It was a sweet sigh that blew warmly against his cheek and made him ache to kiss her again. And that was exactly what he was starting to do when she suddenly pushed him away.

"I—I don't know what came over me. I'm sorry."

He tried to silence her protest with another kiss, but she flitted away from him and walked to the other end of the porch. "This is crazy. I didn't mean to lead you on. You see—" Laurette broke off. How could she identify or describe emotions that were still churning inside herself? She liked him, yes, but it was too soon for her to tamper with romance.

"Tell me what's the matter." His voice was low but still carried a note of command.

"We're friends, Jeff. That's all. I'm not ready for anything else and"—she swallowed dryly—"I don't think I will be for a long time."

A frown marred his face. "That's not what your kiss told me."

She released a wavering sigh. Ah, yes, the kiss. The kiss that had drawn her willingly into a torrent of desire. But the kiss had been a mistake, like a lot of things in her life—like her marriage and her job. She couldn't keep making the same mistake of rushing headlong into things. From now on she was going to go slowly, checking at each step along the way to make sure of firm ground beneath her before taking the next step.

Returning to the swing, she perched on the edge of it and put her palms atop her bare knees. It took her a moment to find the right words. Without looking at him, she began slowly, "I haven't been single long and I admit I'm lonely." It was difficult to continue under his hard scrutiny, but she forced herself to go on. "I'm afraid I responded to your kiss because I'm lonely and need to feel safe and secure with a man," she ended quietly, and was amazed that her voice wasn't shaking when her insides seemed to be trembling like aspen leaves.

"Oh, so it had nothing to do with me?" he asked dryly.

"I didn't mean that!" It had a great deal to do with him. She found him extremely attractive, which was why she had been pulled so easily into the eddy of his kisses. When she was a teenager, and even just a few days ago, she reminded herself, she had fantasized about what it would feel like to kiss him. "But I just can't—can't get involved yet. I think that needs to be clear before we start working together."

Her nerves stretched thin as the silence lengthened between them. The crazy thing about it was she was waiting, breath held, for him to argue with her, to force her to change her mind and draw her back into his arms. For all the certainty in her voice and the wisdom of her words, she didn't feel certain or wise. Instead, she felt a sharp craving to be cradled against him.

"Whatever you say, Etty," he said brusquely.

He was standing in front of her now. Because she couldn't meet his gaze, she looked down at his chest, but even now she was all too aware of the muscular contours of his chest and shoulders.

Without another word he walked away from her, leaving her standing on the porch feeling very much at sea. If she had done the right thing, the smart thing, then why did she feel so unhappy right now?

CHAPTER FOUR

Monday morning Laurette stopped outside the door of the police station and ran a critical eye over her demurely patterned blue silk dress. It was business-like, but didn't attempt to hide her femininity. But then, she reflected wryly, Jeff had already noticed that.

Which was part of the reason she was still standing outside the police station instead of inside. She had not seen or spoken to Jeff in the six days since he'd come to her grandfather's house, and she wasn't sure how he was going to react to her today—or she to him.

Annoyed by her own hesitation, she resolutely pushed the door open. A middle-aged man with a receding hairline looked up from a cluttered desk in the center of the room. Although he was dressed in the same uniform that Jeff wore, this man did not do nearly so much for the outfit.

"Good morning," he said. "Can I help you?"

"I'm Laurette Haily. I'm going to be working here." A quick look around the room revealed the stranger was the only one present. She felt a prickle of disappointment that Jeff wasn't here.

"Oh, yeah, on the computer," he said indifferently. He nodded toward the machine in the corner. "Go ahead and get started. The chief is tied up this morning, but he called to say you'd be coming in. He left some instructions on what to start. They're on the desk by the computer." He returned to his work.

Laurette remained standing by the door. She felt abandoned. Not that she had expected a huge welcoming committee or a speech from the mayor but she *had* thought Jeff would at least be here to explain things to her. Had he made a point of not being present when she arrived? she wondered.

The other man glanced up briefly. "If you need anything, holler."

Slowly she advanced into the room, dropped her purse onto the floor near the computer, and sat down to familiarize herself with its menus. Once she'd switched on the computer, however, she couldn't concentrate. This was a strange office and she needed to feel more at ease in it before she could immerse herself in the job. Abruptly she turned the machine off and walked over to the stranger's desk.

"I didn't catch your name," she said with a friendly smile.

"Walley Stevens." He volunteered nothing further, but merely gazed at her with an expression that registered neither like nor dislike.

She tried again. "How long have you been with the department, Walley?"

"Nine years."

Her eyes drifted over the mountain of papers on his desk. From the looks of it, nine years worth of work was still stacked on his desk. The other desks—there were seven empty ones in all—were much neater. "Are you the only one here today?" she asked pleasantly.

"I'm the desk sergeant. The other men are on patrol or have gone out for target practice with the chief."

Had she imagined it, or was there a derisive undertone to his words, as if he didn't approve of the target practice. Her curiosity was aroused sufficiently for her to dig further. "Do they practice often?"

"Once a month since the new chief took over."

"I see." Walley Stevens, she decided, resented Jeff. Possibly because Walley had been passed over for promotion in favor of Jeff. And clearly Jeff had some ideas about how to run the department that Walley didn't share.

"Do you do the dispatching too?" she asked.

That question earned her a disdainful, "Certainly not."

Laurette glanced over her shoulder at the radio in the corner. "Who does?"

"Mrs. Floyd. She runs the motel on the edge of town and takes care of the dispatching from there."

"I see."

The balding man continued to regard her with an emotionless expression; Laurette made another attempt to be amiable. Nodding toward the work on his desk, she said, "Looks like you're swamped. Once

I get the computer functional, we'll be able to get that stack down in no time."

His eyes widened and he swallowed in a way that made his large Adam's apple bob noticeably, but he said nothing.

Plainly he didn't want to talk to her. Feeling awkward and unwelcome, Laurette dredged up a flimsy smile and retreated back to her corner. "Well, I'd better get to work and start earning my money," she chattered brightly. "Nice meeting you, Walley."

He made no reply.

With that inauspicious beginning to her day Laurette set to work. First she began devising a classification system for the office files. That involved going through the files to see what records were kept and how they were presently arranged.

By noon her hands felt grimy from the musty police records and files, and her pretty silk dress was going limp. Eastern Tennessee's summer heat was beginning to filter in through the open windows, and the ceiling fan that swirled lazily overhead only stirred the warm air.

She was running her fingers through strands of hair that were beginning to float more and more annoyingly around her face when the door opened and several uniformed men poured in.

"You're a hell of a shot, Jeff! How many times did you hit that can anyway?"

"More times than you did, Stockwell," another man answered. "I don't think you came within a mile of it."

"It was a bad day," Stockwell, a rangy man with blond hair, muttered.

She sorted quickly through the crowd, her eyes automatically coming to rest on Jeff. She hadn't known that seeing him again would unleash such a feeling of suppressed excitement and tingling anticipation. She had told him she wanted only his friendship, but the sensations rippling through her body said otherwise.

Jeff noticed her for the first time and inclined his head in a polite greeting. But his eyes looked at her searchingly as if he, too, were remembering that night on the porch and wondering where they stood with each other. "Hello. I see you're hard at work."

"Yes." She swiped at a strand of hair that persisted on falling over her nose.

"Men," Jeff announced to the group around him, "this is our new computer programmer. Laurette Haily, this is Stockwell, Burris, Lawrence, Kendell, and Webber." As he pointed to each man in turn, they mumbled polite words.

Their faces were flushed and even in their uniforms Laurette thought they looked like eager young boys back from a day at the zoo. She smiled at them. "It's good to meet all of you."

Jeff turned back to the men. "You'd better get out in your squad cars and relieve the others."

Moments later the room was empty again except for Jeff, Walley, and Laurette. She felt her heart hammer as he approached her. The burning intensity of their kiss on the porch swing had been slipping steadily from her memory, but his presence brought it back into clear focus and she couldn't help but wonder if Jeff was thinking of it too.

"Let's see what you've done so far," Jeff said, casually drawing up another chair and placing it beside hers.

She explained her plans to him as simply as possible. While she talked she was acutely aware of his nearness. She could see the hard lines of his thighs pressing against the fabric of his slacks and she could smell the leather and starch of his uniform. His shoes were polished to a shiny black. His arms were very close and occasionally brushed against hers.

"You've made a good start," he said when she had finished speaking.

"Thank you." She looked at the computer screen rather than at him. "I thought after I finished with the general office files we could decide how the criminal files should be arranged."

"Sounds good."

"Of course it'll be a few days before I get that far," she continued, knowing that she was chattering aimlessly because she felt unsure of herself with him.

"Have you had lunch?" he asked.

Her tension evaporated. Everything was going to be okay. Jeff wasn't angry with her. "No. Not yet."

He glanced at the large clock on the wall. "Well, you'd better run out and get something before the restaurants get too crowded."

She jerked her head up and found herself staring directly into his unreadable brown eyes. "Aren't you going out to eat?"

"Nope. I brought my lunch." Smiling, he rose and crossed to his desk. "Walley and I always do. Right, Walley?"

The other man grunted something that might have been agreement.

"Oh. Well, in that case . . . ." Picking up her purse, she started toward the door, feeling confused and unhappy even though she kept reminding herself she had wanted to discourage Jeff's interest. Obviously she had succeeded.

Jeff unwrapped his bologna sandwich and watched Laurette walk past the window. Her head was tilted up in an angle that bespoke pride but not arrogance. Her dress moved in time with her quick steps, and he had a nice view of those delectable legs. The sun played hide-and-seek in her soft hair.

Instinctively his mind went back to the moment his lips had tasted hers with delicious inquiry. Their embrace had been all too short.

He sensed a vulnerability about her, a quality that made a man want to open the door for her or bring her a drink, and he wondered if it was the result of her divorce or something she had acquired elsewhere in her life. There was so much about her that he didn't know and that he wanted to learn.

Looking up, Jeff saw that Walley was watching him with his usual glower. "She said she's going to put all the records on the computer. Is that true?" Walley asked.

"Sure. It'll eliminate a lot of paperwork." Jeff's

eyes moved pointedly at the clutter atop Walley's desk.

Abruptly Walley pushed back his chair and rose. "I've got to run some errands during my lunch hour."

Jeff watched the desk sergeant leave. The other men in the police department had viewed Jeff with varying degrees of skepticism when he had become chief. In the eight months since then, he'd won the respect of all the others. All except Walley. The more reforms Jeff instituted, the more Walley seemed to dislike him.

Not that Walley's opinion kept Jeff awake at night. In this business it helped to have a thick skin. And while it was helpful if the men who worked under him liked him, it wasn't imperative as long as they obeyed orders.

Of course things were different where Laurette was concerned. With her it was important that she like him. Very important. But he was going to make sure not to let her know that or she might be frightened off.

At the corner drugstore three blocks from the station Laurette sat at a booth near the fountain. A coney dog and a cherry Coke waited in front of her, but she only picked at her lunch.

From Jeff's impersonal attitude toward her today, it was obvious his interest in her had been quenched, yet her own feelings for him were far more chaotic. She had told herself she wanted to have a working relationship full of the easy camaraderie of old friends. But when she was with him she felt a tension that had much more to do with the fact that he was handsome and virile than the fact that they had once skipped stones across a pond together.

"Mind if I join you?" a female voice inquired.

Laurette looked up to see Belinda standing by her booth balancing a napkin, Coke, grilled cheese, and straw.

"There aren't any other empty seats," Belinda explained.

Laurette nodded and made a be-my-guest gesture while she dabbed at the corner of her mouth with a napkin. With an effort of will she thrust Jeff to the back of her mind. "It gets crowded at noon, doesn't it?" she said in a conversational tone.

"Yes." Belinda slipped into the banquette across from her. The petite woman was wearing a gray seersucker dress that showed off her shapely figure.

Laurette refused to look down at her own sagging blue silk dress. Belinda seemed to be one of those women who could emerge from the smoky beaches of Dunkirk or an atomic war looking unruffled. Laurette's admiration was tinged with envy.

"Isn't today your first day at work?" Belinda asked.

"Yes. Of course this is only a temporary job," Laurette added quickly, and immediately wondered if she had said so to inform Belinda or to remind herself.

The dark-haired woman cupped her chin in her hands and studied Laurette with interest. "Police work has always fascinated me."

"I won't exactly be doing police work," Laurette said. "I'm setting up a computer system for the department."

Belinda was undeterred. "But you'll be right there where everything's happening. You'll know what's going on in this town the minute something interesting happens," she concluded with wistful enthusiasm.

Laurette frowned. She had come to Locust Grove because it was a quiet, serene town away from jarring events. "To tell you the truth, I can't imagine what's going to happen here that would be of much interest."

The other woman shook her head ruefully. "That seems to be the going attitude around here."

"Well, it seems like the logical one based on how dull things have been in the past," Laurette said candidly.

For a moment the two women sat looking at each other, each taking the measure of the other. Laurette wasn't sure how she felt about this pretty woman. She wasn't sure how she wanted to feel, considering that Belinda seemed interested in Jeff. Yet she had already resolved that she would not become involved with Jeff, so how could she resent another woman who was interested in him? She had no ready answer to that question.

"I don't know that Locust Grove has been all that dull in the past," Belinda said evenly. "It's just that things that might have caused a scandal have always been swept under the rug."

Laurette sipped at her cherry Coke and weighed that statement. "That's probably true. And I suspect it'll continue to be that way. Small towns have a way of wanting to keep their secrets hidden." She tilted her head to one side curiously. "Will you answer something for me?"

Belinda smiled. "I don't know, but you can ask."

"What are you doing in Locust Grove? It's obvious that you want to do investigative reporting and that you're interested in police work. You should be in Nashville or Memphis, covering City Hall or the crime beat." The words came out a little blunter than Laurette had intended, and she hurried on before Belinda could answer. "Not that I'm suggesting you leave Locust Grove. On the contrary, with your enthusiasm I'm sure you're a real asset to the paper, but I think you'd be more satisfied in a bigger city."

Belinda's smile deepened. "Thanks for the vote of confidence. And you're right. I would be happier in a big city." She nibbled on her grilled cheese sandwich. "But newspaper jobs aren't easy to get. And times are harder for newspapers than they've ever been before. Quite a few of the large dailies have gone under. I took the only job that was offered," she finished simply.

Laurette grimaced. "Me and my big mouth."

"Don't feel bad." Belinda's face creased into a grin. "I still have hopes of writing a Pulitzer prize—winning story in Locust Grove that will catapult me

68

to national fame and bring *The New York Times* banging on my door."

Laurette chuckled. "I bet you'll just do it too."

This time when they looked at each other Belinda's smile was softer and Laurette felt warmer toward her. They were going to be friends after all.

Both women lapsed into silence for a few moments. When Belinda spoke, it was to say forthrightly, "You're going to like working with Jeff; he's very dedicated. I think he appeals to me because he's one of the few men I know who puts as much into his work as I put into mine."

"I see," Laurette murmured. Belinda was pointing out a side of Jeff she had overlooked—or had not chosen to acknowledge. Any lingering doubt about becoming involved with Jeff should have been erased. It had been a wrenching experience the first time to come in a poor second to her husband's work. It would devastate her if it happened again.

"Of course," Belinda continued with a sad smile, "I'm not sure that Jeff finds my dedication to journalism such an endearing trait. He thinks I see a criminal hiding behind every bush. One time I mentioned to him how suspicious I was of the influx of cars with New York license plates. I was all primed to do an in-depth study about it when he pointed out that it was summer and the height of the tourist season in the Smokies and those were tourists." She laughed lightly. "I'm a general nuisance to him, but he's very patient with me."

"Mmmm." Laurette pinched off a piece of coney. She was still thinking about what Belinda had said about the importance of Jeff's work. Would it always rank first with him? It didn't matter, she told herself, because she wasn't going to get close enough to the fire to get burned a second time.

Across the table Belinda opened her purse and began counting out change. "Uh-oh."

"What's wrong?"

"I'm afraid I don't have enough money. Could you . . . That is . . ."

Laurette laughed. "How much?"

"A dollar."

The money changed hands and Belinda slid out of the booth. "Thanks. I'm glad we had lunch together. I'm really looking forward to seeing you again."

"Me too. Don't forget that you owe me a buck," Laurette called after her, and Belinda waved gaily in response.

Laurette paid for her own meal and started back toward the police station. When she walked through the door Jeff and the man he had introduced as Burris were engrossed in conversation.

"What do you make of that old canning jar?" Burris asked in a low voice.

"It's home brew. No doubt about it."

Home brew! Laurette stopped dead in her tracks.

"Got any ideas who might be making it?" Jeff asked.

She strained to hear.

Burris stretched his short legs out in front of him and pondered. "Jim Casey used to dabble in that a bit, but he's moved to Nashville to live with his

70

daughter. Some of the boys who hang around Cal's Pool Hall might know, but I doubt if they'd tell."

Laurette walked over to Jeff's desk with what she hoped passed for an air of detachment. "Did I hear you say someone around here is making moonshine?"

The two men exchanged glances and suddenly she felt like a six-year-old who'd been caught listening at the keyhole. A flush spread over her cheeks. "Was that supposed to be a secret?"

"I'd prefer that you didn't mention it to anyone," Jeff said tersely.

"Of course not." She stiffened, hurt that he didn't trust her and at the same time feeling guilty because she knew where the moonshine had come from and wasn't telling him.

"We can't have things that go on here being spread around," he added.

"I'm certainly not going to go around town repeating things I hear in confidence," she retorted, stung.

His look of surprise gradually dissolved into a bemused smile and he stretched out a hand, palm upward, in a gesture of peace. "No, of course you aren't. I'm sorry I implied that, Etty," he said softly.

She couldn't be angry at someone who was turning the full attention of his deer-brown eyes on her and smiling in a way that made her knees wobble. And she liked the way his pet name for her rolled easily off his tongue.

"You're not mad, are you?" One dark eyebrow quirked upward questioningly.

"No," she murmured.

"Want to shake on that?"

She put her hand in his and felt strong fingers curl over the delicate bones of her hand. He squeezed gently and his smile mellowed. "That's better. Friends again?"

She wasn't positive, but she thought he'd put just the slightest bit of emphasis on the word *friends,* as if somehow mocking the agreement they'd made to be friends and nothing more. "Friends," she said evenly, and withdrew her hand.

Burris, who had been ignoring the byplay, now joined in again, bringing the conversation back to the business at hand. "Should we make an all-out effort to track down the still?"

Laurette felt herself tensing again. If they began a search, they were bound to find Grandfather's still, and then all hell would break loose. But there was surely no need to be nervous, she told herself. Grandfather wasn't making moonshine anymore. Momentarily she debated the idea of confiding in Jeff about where the homemade liquor had come from. But the memory of Belinda's words that Jeff was an extremely dedicated policeman stopped her. Was he so dedicated that he would feel duty-bound to arrest her grandfather if he knew about his still? That was a chance she didn't want to take. No, since Grandfather wasn't making moonshine any longer it would be best to let this issue die a quiet death.

"We'll do a little looking around," Jeff said. He spoke to Burris, but he was watching Laurette with a narrowness that made her uncomfortable. He was a policeman and trained to know when someone was hiding something. Did he sense that she was keeping something from him? Briskly she walked in the direction of the computer.

"I'd better get back to work," she called over her shoulder as she made her escape.

CHAPTER FIVE

The following week was the busiest one Jeff had had since he'd come to Locust Grove. Perhaps because it was the beginning of the summer and the kids were restless or perhaps because of a wave of unseasonably hot weather, calls poured in. Jeff was busy. Making matters worse, it was now vacation time and a great many tourists were drifting in from the nearby Great Smokey Mountains to see the quaint town, park illegally near the fire hydrants, and snafu traffic by heading the wrong way up the town's only one-way street.

Of course, this was nothing like the pressure he'd known as a detective in Memphis, but it kept him hopping. He came in early and often worked late. At no time did he fail to notice when Laurette came or left, but he had little time to talk to her.

And that was probably for the best anyway, he told himself. She had arrived in Locust Grove only a few days ago, obviously fleeing a traumatic situation both at home and at her job. He wasn't going to rush her, although he was determined to get to know her.

Still, when she walked into the station wearing a

fluttering little dress that whisked around her knees or was cinched in at the middle in a way that showed the slender suppleness of her waist, he was sometimes tempted to shove his work aside and go over to her desk to pursue some old-fashioned flirtation, complete with gazing into her sea green eyes. Luckily he'd so far kept himself from doing anything that foolish.

Friday morning he was filling out a form when Laurette walked in. He produced the brotherly smile he'd been perfecting lately. "Good morning."

"Hi." She hesitated at his desk, then stopped. "You've been really busy lately, haven't you?"

"Yeah." He rested back in his chair and watched her absently run her hand back and forth along the edge of his desk. It was impossible to ignore the unconsciously provocative movements of her hand. Watching her slender fingers move back and forth along the wood made him long to feel those fingers on his body, running up and down the length of his spine. That thought triggered even greater yearnings.

Laurette tucked back a wisp of her silken hair. "Is it always this hectic at the beginning of the summer?"

"I wasn't here last year, but I imagine it is." Her hair looked like filaments of gold, Jeff noted, and he could almost feel them dusting against his cheek. Her lips looked rose-petal soft and her eyes were a dewy green. He felt an almost irresistible urge to take her into his arms and taste her lips.

Just then the door opened and Walley sauntered in. "Good morning," he said unenthusiastically.

"I guess I'd better get to work," Laurette said.

As Jeff watched her leave he was annoyed with Walley for having chosen that moment to arrive. Ten minutes later, however, reason had returned and he was glad for Walley's interruption. He would have made a fool of himself if he'd acted on his impulse and kissed her. He couldn't go too fast with Laurette.

The phone rang and Jeff turned his attention to the problem of calming a distressed mother whose ten-year-old had run away from home after being grounded for a week.

Laurette sat down at her desk, but didn't immediately turn on the computer. Instead, she gazed out the window onto a Main Street that was just awakening for business. Absently she watched Mr. Riley hang a Sale sign in the window of his furniture store while Mr. Everly, who owned the hardware store, propped his door open.

For the past week Jeff had been immersed in his work and seemed to have forgotten that Laurette was even working there. She felt slighted by his indifference. While she hadn't wanted to become romantically involved with him, she wanted and valued his friendship. Yet lately she wasn't even sure she had that. Turning halfway in her chair, she was able to watch him unobtrusively. She could see him sitting at the decrepit old typewriter, hunting and pecking at keys.

He was a terrible typist, but he looked good trying, she thought with a soft smile. His uniform was, as always, flawless, with every crease in place and every brass button shining. His shoulders were hunched forward in a way that gave him the appearance of a linebacker waiting for the tackle. He had nice shoulders too. . . .

Had he really been too busy over the past week to say more than a few words to her? she wondered. He'd certainly been friendly enough to Belinda when she had stopped by yesterday. Jealousy, or something quite a bit like it, reared its ugly head.

Laurette shook her head, bemused by her own thoughts. There it was again—that crazy contradiction of wanting Jeff only as a friend yet resenting any interest he showed in other women. She knew that was wrong, but more and more often the memory of his kisses had intruded and played havoc with reason. Those memories had the power to make her pulse sing and her body ache to be held.

She was startled out of her reveries when the front door opened and Kathy stepped in.

"Hi," she said to the room at large. "Don't get up. I have nothing illegal to report. This is strictly a social visit." Grinning, she crossed to Laurette. "I thought for sure I'd find you locked in one of the jail cells. What other reason could there be for not seeing or hearing from you for over a week?"

Laurette smiled sheepishly. "I'm sorry. I've been meaning to call."

Kathy pulled up a chair. "So what's the story? Do they give you time off for good behavior so we can go shopping?"

Laurette hesitated. She and Jeff had agreed she could keep her own hours, but she'd become so engrossed in setting up a computer filing system that she'd been working eight-hour days. "I can work whatever hours I like but I've—"

"Good! I have a sitter lined up for tomorrow. We can go to Knoxville and spend the day browsing. We'll treat ourselves to a good dinner and maybe a movie. What do you say?" Without giving Laurette a chance to answer, Kathy continued. "After all, you *did* come to Locust Grove to get away from work for a while."

"That's true," Laurette agreed. But this didn't seem like work. She knew that was partly because she was doing it as a favor for Jeff. But she also looked forward to the time she spent at the station. Even when Jeff wasn't around there was a contagious atmosphere of excitement at the police station. And she was frankly intrigued by delving into the police files.

"Can you go shopping tomorrow?" Kathy coaxed, and added in pleading tones, "You're looking at a mother who's desperate to escape for a few hours with another adult."

Laurette smiled. "Since you put it that way, how can I refuse?"

"Terrific!"

"Grandfather and I have a phone now, so I'll call you this evening and we can set up the details," Laurette said.

"That'll be fine. Talk to you later." Kathy rose and started toward the door, stopping along the way to exchange a few teasing words with Jeff.

After Kathy had gone Laurette turned back to her

work. She had almost finished transferring the data from the office files to the computer files. Next she would begin arranging cross-references.

Walley walked up to her desk. "Here are the latest reports," he said tonelessly. "The chief thought you might want to put them directly into the computer." He looked past her as he spoke, as if the whole matter bored him greatly.

"Thank you," she said.

"Yeah." He disappeared out the door.

Laurette had given up trying to make friends with Walley. He clearly didn't want to be her friend. But she had decided it was nothing personal. Walley didn't like Jeff either, although he was respectful toward him. All of the men showed Jeff respect, but the others also liked him.

The way Jeff worked impressed her. Even though Locust Grove was a small town, he was strict about the quality of work. She'd seen him slap more than one sloppy report back on the offending officer's desk with orders to clean it up. Yet even while she admired his professionalism she recognized the same serious attention to detail that Stan had shown. And that disturbed her. Of course she understood that his job was important and she was pleased that he did it well. But she couldn't help wondering if it would always be the most important thing in his life.

Rising, she paced around the empty office, rubbing her hands together in a distracted gesture. Why did it bother her so much that Jeff seemed to have the same flaws as her former husband? He was simply an old friend, not someone she would ever become involved with. Yet even as she told herself that, she was aware of more intimate yearnings seeping to the surface, making her feel as if she were trying to hold the lid on a pot intent on boiling over.

To distract herself with other thoughts she walked back into the separate area of the station that contained four small jail cells. She had never been back here before, and she stopped now to gaze at the metal bars.

Pulling open the door to a cell, she stepped inside and looked around curiously. A break in the bars at the back of the cell led into an adjoining cell and she moved into it, pausing to look up at the iron grill covering the window. Only a few drunks had stayed here since she'd begun work, but there must have been more dangerous criminals here from time to time. And Jeff surely had had to face many a potential killer while on the Memphis police force. In fact, the man who had shot him in the leg had certainly been intending to do more damage.

Her body tensed at the thought of a bullet piercing the flesh of Jeff's leg and exploding against the bone. She had never asked him to tell her about that; she wasn't sure she wanted to know, but every time she saw him limp slightly or wince with a sudden movement, she felt chilled and a lump rose in her throat. She didn't like admitting it, but she knew she felt a deeper compassion for Jeff than she would have felt for almost anyone else.

Distantly she heard the front door of the station open but she didn't look away from the shafts of sunlight streaming in through the grill. It wasn't until she heard a door slam that she swung her attention back to the present. The room she was in, she discovered, did not have a door, only the opening into the other cell.

She moved back into the first cell and saw with a start that an old man was tottering back and forth on his heels and blinking at her with an alcoholic smile. The second thing she saw was the locked cell door.

Taken by surprise, she needed a minute to find her voice. In that time she heard the awful sound of the front door slamming and realized that whoever had put the drunk into the cell had left.

"Hello, ma'am." The drunk tried to tip his hat but that and remaining on his feet was an impossible combination. He ended up slumping backward onto the cell's lone cot.

The full impact of what had happened hit her. She'd been locked in! Dashing to the cell door, she wrapped her fists around the bars and yelled at the top of her voice. "Walley! Get me out of here!"

No answer.

She called again in vain. What if Walley didn't return soon? While she didn't get absolutely hysterical in cramped places, she was enough of a claustrophobic to feel uncomfortable and unhappy and to want out. She raised her voice again. "Help! Can't anyone hear me?"

The drunk blinked. "Is something wrong?" he asked with courtly concern.

Laurette rounded on him. "Of course something's wrong! I've been locked in a jail cell."

"Well, I have too," he pointed out in a polite slur,

81

"but you don't hear me hollering, do you?" Then, realizing that his manners were remiss, he said, "I'm Izzy Percy. And you're—?"

"Laurette Haily," she said distractedly.

"Charmed to meet you."

She turned away from him and rattled fiercely on the door. "Can anyone hear me? Walley!" But no one came and she eventually fell back into silence.

Time dragged on. Izzy passed out and began snoring. Laurette thought it must be two o'clock by now and she hadn't had lunch. Her stomach growled as if in testimony of that fact. When would someone bring food to Izzy? she wondered fretfully and rose to pace the tiny room. What if she and poor Izzy were left here to rot?

She was in the midst of dire speculations of how people would react when her skeleton was found when the front door opened with its customary squeaking. She bounced back to the cell door and shouted, "Get me out of here!"

A second later Jeff rounded the corner and stopped, staring at her in surprise. "What the hell are you doing in there?"

Her eyes snapped indignantly. "I was locked in!"

"Why?"

She waved her hands in an impatient, dismissing gesture. "It was a mistake. Just get me out and I'll explain everything."

"Well, I—" Jeff broke off with a sheepish grin. "I'm afraid I don't have the key."

"What do you mean you don't have the key!"

"Shhh." He was in motion again, advancing to the

cell door and putting his hands over the fingers she had clenched around the bars. "Walley has the key, and it's locked in his desk," he said in soothing tones. "He's not supposed to do that, but he does."

"I'll kill him," she muttered.

"Now, Etty, calm down. You're going to be all right. Walley's gone to the doctor in Mountain Creek, but he'll be back before long." He stroked her fingers comfortingly and looked past her at the sleeping Izzy. Something glinted in his brown eyes.

It suddenly struck Laurette how ridiculous she must look locked up with a boozy cellmate. She stared downward and mumbled, "If you laugh, I'll never speak to you again."

"I'm not laughing."

She ventured a look up at him. Aside from a muscle that twitched suspiciously in one cheek, his expression was appropriately sober.

"What happened?" he asked.

"I was just standing in the adjoining cell and the next thing I knew someone had thrown Izzy in, slammed the door, and left."

"Izzy." Jeff smiled past her to the snoring drunk. The merriment in his eyes was unmistakable now. "Is that your friend's name?"

She gave him a reproving look, yanked her fingers away, and stalked to the tiny, barred window. "You promised not to laugh!"

"Well, yes, I did, but you have to admit it *is* funny."

"I don't happen to think so," she said stubbornly.

Jeff attempted to fight back his smile, but his

brown eyes were so loaded with amusement that it spilled over. The result was that the corners of his mouth kept slanting upward and he had to force them back into a straight line. It would have been easier for Laurette to maintain her solemn, accusing stare if he hadn't looked so boyishly tickled.

"C'mon, Etty, don't take it so seriously," he cajoled, and his face broke into a roguish smile.

She folded her arms across her chest and turned away from him.

"It'll go easier on you if you cooperate with the police, ma'am." His voice had softened to a husky burr that sent her pulse skittering out of control. How could any man seduce her from behind the bars of a jail cell? she wondered dazedly. Especially while a drunk snored nearby. But somehow Jeff was. Above the scent of Izzy's sour mash she could detect Jeff's musky cologne and smell the fresh polish on his shoes. What could possibly be so sexy about shoe polish? she wondered. Well, maybe shoe polish wasn't sexy, but *Jeff* was and she couldn't prevent herself from stealing a glance at him. He was still smiling and it was the most unabashedly provocative expression she'd ever seen. Her heart raced faster.

The front door opened and Jeff glanced over his shoulder. "I believe the cavalry has arrived. Wait right there."

What choice did she have? Pushing Izzy's feet out of the way, she sat down on the edge of the cot. She didn't know how much longer she could have remained standing anyway. Watching Jeff with his warm, enticing smile had made her legs feel weak.

Jeff reappeared and unlocked the door. "You're free to go, ma'am," he said in his best *Dragnet* voice. "We'll just need you to sign a few forms at the front desk."

She pushed herself off the wafer-thin mattress and started toward the door. With a sticky Southern-belle smile, she asked, "Could I borrow your gun while I go chat with Walley?"

Jeff chuckled, put his arm around her, and whisked her out into the office. "On the assumption you'd feel that way, I sent Walley out on an errand. Now I'm going to take you out for a picnic up in the hills to help you recover from this traumatic experience."

A picnic? She hadn't been up in the hills since she'd been home, and she hadn't had a picnic there since tenth grade. The idea held enough nostalgic appeal for her to let Jeff propel her across the room and outside. He opened the door on the passenger's side of his gray sedan and she slid in. Her indignation at being locked in the cell was replaced by pleasant memories of the summer days she'd spent exploring the hills around Locust Grove. Odd that she hadn't been back up into the hills since her return; she was glad Jeff was going to correct that.

"We'll pick up something to eat on the way," he said.

He stopped at a small grocery store on the edge of town and they went inside together. The counter man sliced the ham for Jeff while she picked out a loaf of French bread and some cheese.

Ten minutes later they were bumping along a lane

that looked familiar. She couldn't recall where it led, but she had a vague memory of having ridden her bicycle along it with the rest of the gang. "Where are we going?"

He turned to give her a mysterious smile. "It's a surprise."

A few minutes later Jeff parked the car amid the tall grass and weeds by the side of the road and they began walking toward a stand of redbud trees. Squirrels chattered at them from the branches as they made their way up a slope. Yes, she had been here before, Laurette realized. But while her sense of recognition grew stronger, the recollection remained lost in the mists of her memory. Then they came to a clearing in the trees and Laurette felt as if someone had turned back the pages and she was looking into yesterday.

In front of her the old gristmill remained standing, although its stone sides were crumbling and the waterwheel beside it was half gone. But it had been half gone when Laurette was a child. The stream that had once powered the waterwheel lapped over mossy stones on its way down to the valley. A smile touched her lips. How many times had she and the others tried to cross those mossy stones and gotten a cold dunking for their trouble?

"Do you remember this place?"

Jeff's words pulled her out of her reverie. "Yes. It was our gang's 'secret' meeting place." She laughed softly. "Or as secret as anything can be among a bunch of noisy ten-year-olds."

He chuckled and crossed the clearing to a sourwood tree beside the mill. There he began spreading out a blanket he'd brought from the car. She followed and stood on tiptoe to pick one of the tree's cream-colored blossoms. While Jeff unpacked the food she set the flower carefully in the center of the blanket. Then she cut the cheese and he broke off pieces of bread.

"The last time I remember being here with you, you were about thirteen and you fell into the stream and almost caught your death of pneumonia," Jeff said.

"I was *pushed* in by Mary Jane." She looked at him slyly. "You remember Mary Jane, don't you? As I recall, she was your heartthrob in high school. I don't know what you saw in her. She had an IQ of a potato and if she ever said anything besides 'Like wow!' I never heard it."

He laughed and reached across her for a slice of cheese. "An adolescent boy's tastes aren't the most discriminating. Speaking of old flames," he added with a significant look at her, "what about that dark-eyed Spanish teacher you had a crush on? The guy was twice your age and he was married."

Laurette threw a crust of bread to the chattering squirrels. "I did have a little crush on Mr. Ortez," she admitted.

"A little crush," he repeated with a disbelieving laugh. "You worshipped the ground he walked on."

She looked at the ground with a reflective smile. "Yeah, I did. I slept with his picture under my pillow," she confessed. "And I cried for three days when he was transferred to another school. I thought

I'd never recover, but two months after he left I'd forgotten all about him. Funny how things that mean so much to you as a kid don't mean a thing later on. Values sure do change."

They continued to make light conversation and laughed easily while they sat on the blanket and ate. It was an informal meal, but the food tasted delicious. Or perhaps it was that being out in the open air had whetted their appetites. They both ended up reaching for the last piece of bread. Her hand closed over it at the same time as his did and neither one would let go of it.

"You should be a gentleman and give it to me," Laurette said with a smothered laugh.

"Hah! You should be a lady and let me have it."

He wrestled her from a sitting position onto her back. "Bully," she said between gasps of laughter. At first she was intent only in hanging on to the bread, but then she found herself looking up into his face and entirely different thoughts ran through her mind. She sensed that he felt it too. The playful wrestling stopped and they were both very still.

Jeff's face was inches from hers. She felt the warmth of his breath on her skin and saw the laughter die in his eyes and desire kindle in its place. His hands continued to hold hers pinned above her head and his body covered hers. She was conscious of the firm weight where his thighs meshed against hers and felt his chest thumping above her own. Every inch of him was hard and masculine.

Slowly he loosened his grip on her hands. She could have pushed against him as a sign she wanted up, but when she lifted her hands it was to run her fingers through his thick brown hair. As her eyes remained fixed on his, she saw them darken with intent.

His arms encircled her and pulled her tightly against him. She went willingly, savoring the fresh masculine smell of his skin and the soft motions of his lips on hers. He rained a light shower of kisses on her mouth, followed by more intense, questing ones that grew in intensity until Laurette was aware of nothing in the world except his body. His tongue expressed his passion, flitting into her mouth and exploring its recesses.

His body was as firm and muscled as she had imagined it would be, but his hair was soft and she let her fingers trail through it, creating tiny corrugations. All the while her lips mingled with his in a sweet, erotic dance. While his body became more taut, hers softened with growing desire.

Whatever reasons she'd had for not wanting to become involved with Jeff Murray had blown away like a mountain mist. All she knew now was that his body had a sinuous strength and it felt utterly right pressed against her own. Her anticipation sharpened when his hands began to move toward her breasts with clear intent.

Laurette willingly let herself glide into those feathery currents of feeling, aching for him to touch her with greater intimacy and willing his lips and tongue to continue flirting with hers. Her own hands slid from his hair down to the strong line of his back and massaged it.

With a hoarse sound of satisfaction he pulled her even closer against him and his mouth moved down to plant a circle of kisses around her throat before ending up at her ear. There he explored the dainty crevices with the moist tip of his tongue. A delicious thrill ran up and down her spine. While his mouth claimed one part of her his hands were working a miracle of their own as they crept over the full swell of her breasts and lingered there. All the while the warm weight of his body covered hers, exciting a thousand wondrous feelings to life.

"Etty?" he said hoarsely.

"Mmmm?"

He raised up on one elbow. "Just exactly where are we headed?"

She fluttered her lashes open and looked at him. His brown eyes were dark with passion and his mouth was soft and full from her kisses. His chest moved in and out in time to his ragged breathing and his cheeks were flushed. Languidly she lifted a finger and traced around his mouth. "You mean you don't know?" she whispered breathlessly. Lacing her fingers behind his neck, she tugged him back down to her and drew him into a deep, passionate kiss.

For a time he was a willing participant, but moments later he pulled back again. "I'm afraid I do know, but this is hardly the place." As he looked at her she could see he was struggling to control his desire.

Laurette's eyes moved to the empty clearing. It seemed the most isolated place in the world, but somewhere in the distance she heard a dog bark and she realized a hunter or someone exploring the woods could easily happen upon them. And Jeff *was* the chief of police.

Slowly she sat up and touched her fingers to her hair. "I—I guess you're right."

He sat up beside her and touched her face gently. She could see the longing in his eyes and knew that his desire, like hers, had not been satisfied. But the rational side of her was glad he had stopped them before things progressed too far.

CHAPTER SIX

Once Laurette had returned to her grandfather's house she was even more relieved that Jeff had called a halt to their lovemaking. She already knew how tied up he could become with his work and she didn't want to get involved with another man whose first priority was his job. She'd read somewhere that divorced women often chose men who had exactly the same shortcomings as their ex-husbands, but she was not going to make that mistake. Then how had she let herself fall so willingly into Jeff's arms this afternoon? The memory of his kisses and caresses brought sharp longings back to life.

"I mustn't think about that," she chided herself aloud. But it was hard to ignore the desire still simmering deep in her veins. To get Jeff off her mind she decided to busy herself weeding the wild tangle of a garden, something that she'd been putting off for several days.

She dressed in a pair of old cut-off jeans and a gingham blouse that tied at her midriff and went out into the garden. Wading into the midst of the thick growth, she began yanking up chickweed and sumac and tossing them onto a pile to wither. She worked feverishly, as if she could exorcise her demons by putting all her energy into her task.

It didn't work. Visions of Jeff continued to dominate her thoughts. Yes, she was attracted to him, but before she invested her emotions again she wanted to be very sure. Yet not an hour ago she had thrown herself into Jeff's arms as if he were the only reality on a planet of illusion. What had possessed her to do that?

Suddenly a male voice intruded into her thoughts. "Hey, you're pulling at those weeds as if they're your personal enemies."

Her grandfather's house sat on a corner, so the backyard was bordered by a sidewalk on one side. Still bent to her task, Laurette brushed back her hair and looked up at the man who was leaning casually against the white picket fence. Reddish hair capped a delicate face that looked familiar. Frowning, she studied him more closely and tried to place him.

"Remember me? Howard?"

She came straight up. "Oh, my gosh! Little Howie."

"Howard," he corrected with a horrified look and a quick glance around to make sure no one had overheard.

A smile settled on her face as she headed toward Howard. "Well, whatever you call yourself now, it's good to see you."

"It's good to see you too. I didn't know you were in town."

"I'm here only for a short while," she explained.

"Do you still live in Locust Grove?" As she stepped closer to the fence she saw that Howard was wearing a pair of white shorts and a blue and white striped polo shirt. He had a nice tan and had filled out far better than she would have expected. She'd always liked him. He had been the youngest boy in her class and the smallest, but he'd always had the sweetest smile. He still had a nice smile.

"I'm still here," he said easily. "I teach art at the high school."

"Really?" She rested her grass-stained hands atop the picket fence. "I remember how you were always doodling. You used to tell everyone you were going to be a famous artist."

"I'm working at it. I paint during the summer. A gallery in Atlanta displays my work."

She raised one eyebrow. "Congratulations. That's very impressive."

He grinned sheepishly. "Thanks."

How well she remembered that toe-scuffing, "aw-shucks" look. Some things about Howard might have changed, but in other ways he was still little Howie, just as Jeff was part handsome stranger, part old friend.

"I'd like to see some of your paintings," she said.

He looked pleased. "Come over anytime. I live just a block away in the old Crawley house. My studio's out back in a small barn."

They chatted for several minutes more before he glanced past her at the morass of weeds and chuckled. "I'd better let you get back to your job. It looks like you've got your work cut out for you."

Once he was gone she returned to weeding, but she felt calmer now and she could look at what had happened this afternoon more objectively. Okay, so she had let herself get carried away with Jeff. That was forgiveable. After all, he was a handsome, virile man and she liked him. But she would be much more careful from now on not to let her passion skitter out of control. Friends, that's what she and Jeff were going to be. Absentmindedly she pulled up some Queen Anne's lace and pitched it onto the heap. Putting her hand on the small of her back, she straightened carefully.

Moving slowly, she headed into the house to take a bath and rub ointment on her aching muscles. Grandfather was just coming up from the basement when she entered the house. His hands were full of canning jars and when he saw her his face became a study in guilt. He threw a quick glance over his bony shoulder as if weighing the advisability of fleeing back down into the basement.

Laurette didn't give him the chance. "What are those for?" she demanded.

Never one to remain on the defensive long, Grandfather was already stiffening rebelliously. "I was fixin' to throw them in the trash." Suiting action to word, he clumped across to the wastebasket and tossed them in. "There, does that satisfy you?" he asked testily.

Oh, dear. She pulled out a pattern-back chair and slumped into it. "You're running another still, aren't you?" The words were a weary formality; she already knew the answer.

"What I do is my own damn business."

"Not if it's illegal, it isn't. Then it becomes the business of the state police and the federal government and the sheriff and local police and probably any other law enforcement official you happen to think of." She was too tired to deal with this at the moment, but she knew that ignoring problems wouldn't make them go away.

Doggedly she continued. "Listen, I don't know how much money you're making at this moonshine business, but it can't be worth it. You can get into tons of trouble! The police already know someone in the area is making mash, so it's only a matter of time before they find the still and *you* with it."

He stood with military erectness, his jaw thrust out. "They won't find it."

She rolled her eyes in exasperation. "How can you be so positive?"

"Because I've got it where no one will ever find it."

"Oh?" A cunning thought crept into her mind. With her most innocent smile she asked, "And where's that?"

"Humph. I'm not going to tell *you*. You'd be up there takin' the thing apart piece by piece."

She pounced. "Up there! So it's up in the mountains somewhere. Is it close to the house?"

He hitched up his suspenders and looped his wrinkled fingers around them. "Mebbe so, mebbe not."

Seeing the glint in her grandfather's eye, Laurette realized he was enjoying this cat-and-mouse game. As stubborn as he was, she knew he'd never tell her where he had relocated the still. She'd just have to

96

make it her business to find out, which shouldn't be too hard to do. She'd simply follow him sometime when he left the house; sooner or later he was bound to lead her to the still. He might be spry, but he was no spring chick, so logic told her the contraption couldn't be too far away.

"You're home early today, aren't you?" he asked.

Now that she had a plan she let him get away with changing the subject. "Yes." Gingerly she rubbed her hands up and down her sore back.

"How come?" he asked.

"It's a long story."

His white caterpillarlike eyebrows lowered in a frown as he watched her massage her back. "Did you hurt yourself on the job?"

"No. I did this pulling weeds." When he continued staring at her she found herself explaining. "I needed an outlet for my energy; I don't get much exercise at work."

He snorted. "I don't know why you're working at the police station anyhow. I thought you came 'ere to rest up."

Laurette didn't have a solid explanation for why she was working there when she had come here to escape computer work. "I'm doing it to help out," she said vaguely.

"You're sort of sweet on that Murray boy, aren't you?"

"Jeff?" she said with an utter casualness that didn't do justice to the way her heart quickened at the sound of his name.

"Yeah, that's the one."

97

She shrugged. "We work together, that's all. We're not dating or anything." Naturally she didn't mention what had almost taken place in the hills this afternoon. Grandfather was just old-fashioned enough to believe in shotgun weddings.

He nodded his approval. "That's good. I don't want that policeman snooping around the place even if he is pitchin' woo at you."

Laurette laughed at the quaint expression. "Jeff's not snooping around and neither is he 'pitching woo' at me. We're friends; that's all."

"He's still a policeman," Grandfather said, as if that in itself were unforgivable.

Laurette pushed her hair away from her face with the back of her grass-stained hand. "You don't have anything to worry about. He's not going to be coming to see me again," she said.

"Good!"

She didn't respond to that. "I think I'll go take a bath now." Walking up the stairs, she admitted to herself that she didn't share her grandfather's relief that Jeff wouldn't be coming around anymore.

Laurette didn't go shopping the next day. "I'm really sorry," she explained to Kathy on the phone, "but I sprained my back and I'm just not up to it."

Kathy took it in good grace. "We'll make it some other time. Maybe next week."

"Sure."

"You stay in bed and rest."

"I intend to." In truth Laurette was enjoying the role of invalid. Even Grandfather had been solicitous this morning, bringing more and more pillows until she thought she'd drown in them. But she'd drawn the line when he'd come shuffling in with the castor oil and a teaspoon. She didn't care if it was "Good for what ails you," she wanted no part of it.

Fortunately Grandfather had not persisted and had left the house. Laurette suspected he'd gone to check his still, but she hadn't felt up to following him.

To occupy herself she'd dug out a book Kathy had loaned her that showed a couple in a torrid embrace on the front cover. She read two chapters, then slipped the book under her pillow and sank back among the cushions on the sofa. Kathy had said the book was "guaranteed to raise your blood pressure," but Laurette didn't need a book to do that. Just thinking about the passion that had erupted yesterday between herself and Jeff brought color to her cheeks. She didn't know how she was going to be able to go back to work and act as if nothing had happened.

To make matters worse, since she had made no attempt to stop him, she saw no reason why Jeff would not be thinking that she wanted to go beyond a casual friendship. She was going to have to make it clear to him that she hadn't changed her mind.

Her thoughts wandered off in another direction and she soon sank into sleep. She didn't awaken until sometime later to the sound of a knock on the door.

Groggily she lifted up on her elbows. "Come in."

* * *

Jeff stepped into the living room and smiled at Laurette, who was lying on the sofa.

Her eyes widened and her mouth formed a circle of surprise. "Oh! I—I wasn't expecting you."

"I ran into Kathy after work and she told me you were sick," he said cheerfully. Laurette looked very sexy when she first woke up, he decided. As he crossed to the divan he saw a book peeping from beneath her pillow. He pretended not to notice, but it would have been impossible to miss that cover. Although it was a long way from shocking him, it would have certainly made his maiden aunt blush.

"I was on my way home from work and thought I'd stop in. How are you feeling?" he asked, stifling a smile as the book began slipping farther toward the floor.

"Okay. I hurt my back pulling weeds," she said in a small voice and indicated a chair.

He sat down. "I'm sorry to hear that." Laurette looked demure and pretty lying there in a pink cotton gown that was covered with rosebuds. A cover was pulled up primly above her breasts, but he could still see the appealing outline they made beneath the cover. Her eyes were a forest green today and her honey gold hair was tousled. She looked innocent and seductive at the same time. He decided it was a powerful combination.

"Were you busy at work today?" She didn't look at him as she fidgeted with the covers.

He had the impression she wasn't quite comfortable with him, but he didn't know why. Things had been fine when he'd dropped her off yesterday. Perhaps she felt self-conscious in her nightgown. "No busier than usual." At that moment the book slipped out from under the pillow and thudded to the floor. Laurette reached for it, but Jeff was quicker. He picked it up with a devilish grin. "Been reading, I see."

She looked guilty, then defiant, and finally whimsically amused. "Yes." Her laughter became musically husky. "I don't suppose you'd believe me if I told you Kathy gave me the book and I was reading it only because I had nothing else to do?"

He flipped through the book. "Nope."

"Want to borrow it when I'm through?" she asked saucily.

He liked it when she smiled like that. The faintest hint of a dimple played in her right cheek and her eyes shimmered like a rolling green ocean. "I'll wait for the movie." As he returned the book to her his attention was drawn to the silken disarray of her hair. "Think you'll be able to come to work tomorrow?"

"Why? Is Walley pining away for me?" she asked pertly.

Their bantering over the book had smoothed their awkwardness and she seemed at ease with him again. Good, he thought with satisfaction. "No, *I'm* pining away for you to get back to work on the computer program. I've been so busy lately, I haven't had a chance to ask you how it's coming."

"I've almost finished the office files except for listing the unclaimed property in the stolen property room. I went out there the other day." She tucked back a wisp of hair and made a face. "What a disaster area!"

"It's a mess," Jeff agreed. He'd told Walley a dozen times to get it straightened out, but so far without results. Tomorrow he'd present the order a little more forcefully.

"Oh, I almost forgot, I brought you something." He reached into his pocket and pulled out a small white box with the words "Wright's Confectioners" scrolled across the top in gold. You always liked Wright's fudge."

Her eyes grew emerald with delight. "You remembered!"

"Of course," he said matter-of-factly. Now that he'd met Laurette again, he was finding he remembered a lot of things about her. And there were lots more things he wanted to know.

"I can't believe you remembered," she murmured as she reverently lifted the lid and looked down at the little shell-shaped pieces of fudge.

He shrugged modestly.

"How sweet."

She was looking at the candy, but he hoped she meant him. Since yesterday he at least had good reason to hope, even to expect. And the next time he kissed her he was going to be sure it was in a place private enough so they could finish what they had started.

"Here, have one." She handed him a piece of fudge, then popped one into her own mouth. "It's heavenly," she sighed.

She didn't notice that the covers had slipped to her

waist, but Jeff did, and he had a tantalizing view of her filmy nightgown.

He heard noises below but assumed it was her grandfather and paid little attention until he saw Laurette tense visibly. "Should I go check on who that is?" he asked.

"No! It's only Grandfather. He must have come in through the outside entrance to the basement." Laurette peeked up at him from beneath long silky lashes, then looked away.

He watched quizzically, uncertain what to make of this new shift in her mood. He could hear the old man coming up the basement stairs as well as the sound of glass clinking.

Laurette's face froze in anticipation. When a door that led up from the basement opened in the next room, she called, "Grandfather, we have company. Jeff Murray is here to see me. You remember him, don't you? The policeman?"

Jeff heard a few words of mumbling, as if the old man were talking to himself, then more shuffling and the sound of his return to the basement. Odd. Jeff looked at Laurette curiously. "Did I scare him off?"

"No, of course not." Her hands fluttered around on the covers and she avoided his eyes.

He didn't believe her. "What's wrong?"

"Well—" She lowered her voice and picked lint off the cover. "Grandfather's become, you know, a little peculiar."

Jeff relaxed. So that was it. She wasn't telling him anything he didn't already know. "I'm sorry to hear that," he said sincerely.

"It's nothing serious, but he sometimes avoids people. He's used to being alone, I suppose," she concluded with an indulgent smile. "He'll probably even be glad to see me go."

"I doubt that," Jeff said, and had to make a deliberate effort not to betray how unsettling it was to hear her talk about leaving.

CHAPTER SEVEN

Shortly after noon the next day Laurette was the only one at the police station. Jeff was answering a call and Walley was in the stolen property room, which was located across the back alley from the police station, sorting and cataloguing the items and making it obvious he disliked the task.

Laurette was just as glad Jeff was gone. First the picnic by the gristmill and then the candy when she was sick. It was sweet, yes, but Jeff was behaving more and more like a man courting a woman. And that wasn't what she wanted.

Or at least she didn't think that was what she wanted. But every time she thought about their interlude beside the gristmill, yearning overtook logic and she wasn't at all sure what she wanted. One thing was certain: Jeff Murray had the power to confuse her.

The front door opened and Belinda entered and looked around. "Do you know when Jeff will be back?"

Laurette glanced up from the computer. "No."

"Oh." The pretty reporter remained standing in the doorway as if unsure what course to take.

"Do you want me to give him a message?" Laurette asked, then added quickly, "Unless it's personal and you'd rather not tell me." She tried to appear indifferent, but she was avidly curious.

Sighing, Belinda shook her head. "It's not personal, but if I left a message he'd probably toss it into the wastebasket and chalk it up as another example of my hallucinating a network of hidden crime when there's a perfectly innocent explanation."

Laurette smiled, surprised at how relieved she felt that this was a business call. "Now you've aroused my curiosity. What are you talking about?" Her still-sore back was beginning to ache from sitting hunched over the computer, and she was glad for a diversion.

"This is probably silly, but yesterday I was driving down West Lane—I was down there to do a story on old Mrs. Crosley, who makes quilts—and a car shot out of an overgrown lane and darn near hit me. The driver was going like a bat out of hell, pardon the expression, and I barely saw his face, but I could see enough to realize it wasn't anyone I knew."

Laurette tilted her head politely. "So?"

Belinda shrugged. "I suppose it's nothing, but doesn't it seem odd to you for a stranger to be out in that neck of the woods? I mean, it's pretty isolated and most of the traffic is local. Besides that, the lane the person came out of was overgrown and led to a deserted shack."

"Did you drive back to the shack?"

"Yes."

Laurette leaned forward on her chair, her interest quickening. "See anything?"

"Not exactly."

"What's that mean?" she probed.

Belinda looked over her shoulder, then confessed in a small voice, "I turned chicken once I got there. It was almost dark and the place looked so eerie and I thought, What if someone's in there? I decided against going in and finding out."

"I can understand that." Laurette glanced at her watch and made a quick decision. "But it's broad daylight now. Why don't you and I drive out there and take a look around?"

Belinda looked as if she didn't dare believe her good luck. "You mean you'll go with me?"

"Sure. Just let me turn off my computer." Laurette pressed the keys to store the information, then flipped the Off switch and rose with a smile. "Ready?"

They took Belinda's blue hatchback and headed down West Lane. The road they followed out of town changed from blacktop to rock and finally to dirt. They ended up in an area that was, as Belinda had said, not the sort of place where one expected to meet anyone but the local residents. It was a good mile from downtown to West Lane, but some far-sighted city planner in days gone by had incorporated a huge area of farmland into the city, probably to increase the tax base. Anyway, it was within the jurisdiction of the Locust Grove police.

After they'd been on the dirt road a few hundred

yards, Belinda braked and peered at the overgrown fencerow. "The lane is along here somewhere. The weeds are so thick, I may have trouble finding it."

"Can you see the house from the road?"

"No."

Laurette studied her surroundings. The road was deserted. Around them lay the rolling hills that eventually blended into the hazy Smokies to the east. She felt safe enough in the daytime, but she could well understand why Belinda hadn't wanted to explore by herself at dusk.

"Here it is." Having overshot the weed-choked lane, Belinda had to back up to aim the car into it. A rusting barbed wire fence tilted precariously and the fenceline was a row of jumbled brambles. Belinda inched the car carefully down the bumpy lane for a quarter of a mile before rounding a bend.

Laurette blinked at the somber house that lay before her. It was everything that Belinda had said and less. The weathered gray boards on the front porch curled up at the ends and some of the windows were covered with panes too dirty to see through. Other windows stood empty and gaping. The word *haunted* came to mind, and suddenly Laurette felt prickly at the thought of going into the house.

"Belinda, I—"

Her companion chuckled. "I know. You suddenly remembered that today is the day you sort your socks and you have to rush right home and do that. I was thinking the same thing myself."

Knowing that she wasn't the only coward in the crowd gave Laurette a reckless feeling of courage, or at least a bravado that would pass for courage. "We're acting like a couple of kids who're afraid of their shadows. Come on. There aren't any cars here, so we're obviously alone. We can just take a quick peek through the windows and leave."

"You're right."

Belinda stopped the car and they both got out. A sea of chickweed and pennyroyal came up to their thighs and they used their hands like oars to push back the stocking-snagging weeds.

"This is about what my front yard looks like," Belinda commented, but the words didn't sound as light as intended.

When they reached the house Laurette felt glass crunch beneath her feet that had fallen out of the window. She looked through the empty frame into a tiny room with discolored wallpaper on the walls. The floor was bare except for a few rusting tin cans that suggested a hobo had stayed there in the past.

"Nothing here," Laurette said in the quiet murmur one might use in church—or in a graveyard at night.

They moved on to the next window. Its glass was still intact, but Laurette could see through the murky pane enough to recognize a room very like the first. Rags of curtains hung from the windows.

"Should we go inside?" Belinda asked.

"I don't know," Laurette whispered. The silence around them was broken only by the drumming of a distant ruffled grouse and the chatter of red squirrels. Even those familiar sounds were somehow disquieting. "The floor might not be stable." But that was only part of her reluctance to go inside.

"That's true."

Laurette crept around the corner and looked into the kitchen window. Cabinets were falling from the walls and the stove had been ripped out, leaving pipes exposed. Belinda started to move on, but Laurette caught her arm. "Look," she breathed.

A door stood ajar and steps descended down into a dark basement. Leading toward the basement was a clear trail of footprints in the dust. Large footprints. The hair came up on the back of Laurette's neck.

"Sh-should we go inside?" Belinda asked thickly.

Laurette stared at her. "Are you crazy? Whoever left those prints could still be inside. Let's get out of here!"

"Good idea."

They both darted back to the car with more speed than grace. Once inside the hatchback they began locking doors.

"It could be nothing at all," Belinda pointed out unsteadily.

"Yeah, well I'll let someone else find out," Laurette muttered, looking around uneasily at the tangle of huckleberry bushes, scrub oaks, and tough little locusts forming a grove behind the house. It would be so easy for someone to hide there. What if someone were watching them at this very minute? Her skin began to crawl. "Let's go."

Belinda started the car, turned it around quickly, and headed back down the lane.

It was only when they were a comfortable distance from the house that Laurette wondered aloud. "What would anyone be doing in the basement?"

"I don't know," Belinda said, "but as soon as we get back to town, let's find a policeman and send him out here to find out."

"A policeman sounds like the very person." Far better than *her*, Laurette reflected with a glance over her shoulder. What if there had been someone lurking in the basement? Visions of ax murderers and late night horror shows flitted through her mind, and she felt chilled even though the temperature was in the eighties.

They passed from the dirt road onto the rock and then to the blacktop. Belinda glanced around as they drove into town. "Where are all the police cars anyway? There's never a cop around when you need one."

"There's one." Laurette pointed toward the black and white cruiser parked in front of the café. A uniformed officer was emerging, inserting a toothpick in his mouth as he walked. "And there's Stockwell."

Belinda made an illegal U-turn and whipped in beside him.

The tall blond-haired officer leaned down and smiled in through the open car window. "Hello, ladies."

Belinda wasted no time on pleasantries. "We've just come from West Lane and there's something funny going on out there."

She paused for breath and Laurette picked up the story. "There's an old abandoned house out there.

111

Belinda saw someone coming out of the lane yesterday driving like crazy and we went out there today and saw footprints inside that lead to the basement."

He looked from one to the other curiously. "That's it?"

"Yes." Laurette ran a hand through her hair. It suddenly occurred to her that the facts that had seemed so unnerving while she and Belinda had actually been at the house sounded rather ordinary now. So what if they'd seen a car and footprints? The footprints were logical, since they already knew someone had been there yesterday. That person could have been scavenging for junk or possibly owned the property.

Belinda must have been thinking the same thing, for she sounded almost defensive when she said, "It's something that should at least be investigated."

Stockwell chuckled. "Have you two been telling each other ghost stories?"

"You can at least go out and check," Belinda said crisply, but a flush was creeping into her cheeks.

"Okay, I'll take a run out there sometime this afternoon." He tipped his hat. "Good afternoon, ladies." He sauntered lazily toward his car.

"I feel like a fool," Laurette mumbled.

"Yeah. I guess we did get a little carried away." Belinda laughed shortly. "And you're going to get a heck of a ribbing from the guys at the police station if Stockwell goes out there and doesn't find anything unusual."

"I probably will," Laurette agreed ruefully, and plucked a cocklebur from her raspberry poplin dress, then another one. "My hose are shredded and I've got bits of weeds all over my dress."

"I'm sorry," Belinda offered.

"Don't apologize. It was *my* idea to go out there." She plucked another cocklebur from the dress and tossed it out the window. "But I don't want to go back to the office looking like this. Why don't you drop me off at my grandfather's house?"

"Sure."

Ten minutes later Laurette had changed out of her rumpled dress into a pair of comfortably faded jeans and a shirt that was so large it waffled around her and hung to her thighs. From the kitchen window she could see the mountains in full bloom and she paused a moment to drink in the view. The rhododendrons created scattered drops of pink and rose and lavender among the green of the hills.

As a child she had strolled the gentler slopes with her mother, peeking among the delicate mosses and maidenhair ferns in search of elves. Later she had clambered over the steeper hills with boisterous young companions, jumping across Blackberry Creek from stone to mossy stone, happy just to be alive. And among the companions tumbling down grassy hillsides beside her had been Jeff.

Laurette sighed. She had come to Locust Grove to forget the past and to plan her future. Yet the present was what filled her thoughts and Jeff was very much a part of that present.

It had begun as a renewing of an old friendship at the gas station, but it had quickly become more. She liked his smile, admired the easy way he carried his authority, and felt a womanly response to his presence. But Locust Grove was only a way station for her between jobs, and soon she would be leaving. She didn't want to feel attracted to him. If he weren't so persistent, perhaps she could have ignored her attraction to him.

But Jeff was persistent. He'd wrapped her in kisses on the picnic and his thoughtfulness in bringing her the candy had touched her deeply. He was making it difficult for her to be indifferent, which was exactly what he intended to do, she realized. She had told him in the beginning that she didn't want to become involved, yet he was ignoring her wishes. Laurette felt a flutter of resentment at that realization. Not only was she fighting conflicting emotions within herself, but she was also having to maintain her resolve in the face of Jeff's constant attention.

A movement caught her eye outside. Through the back window she saw Grandfather emerge from the shed, cross the backyard, and disappear into the alley behind their house, carrying a large sack of sugar. Her pulse quickened. Obviously he was headed for the still. This was the opportunity she'd been waiting for. With any luck he'd lead her to the still.

She set out after him, letting herself out the back gate into the alley where coal wagons and ice trucks had once clattered. Two blocks ahead she saw Grandfather crossing the road into a field a-tangle with blackberry briars. Beyond the small field the landscape rose quickly and folded back on itself to form a series of rolling hills. Here and there on the rockier hillsides she could see dark patches that she knew were caves.

As she continued down the alley, a cat darted out from behind a garage into her path and tripped her. By the time she had regained her balance and retied her tennis shoe Grandfather was halfway across the field. For an old man he certainly could move fast, she marveled. Laurette unsuccessfully tried to increase her speed, but she wasn't used to walking in the tall Bermuda grass.

A few minutes later she crossed the road into the field. By then her grandfather had disappeared over a hill. Her shoelace came untied and she almost fell again. "To heck with it," she muttered, and took off her shoes, carrying them as she began to run barefoot up the hill. When she reached the top she paused to catch her breath. Below her lay a pretty green valley with a small stream winding through it. She scanned the hillsides, but didn't see her grandfather. Where could he have gone? Had he followed the stream around the side of the hill, or had he already climbed over the top of the second hill?

From somewhere behind her she heard whistling. She glanced over her shoulder and saw a man coming up the slope toward her. It was Howard. With a sigh of resignation she waited for him to join her. She'd have to find the still another day.

"Are you out for a walk?" Howard asked when he reached her.

"Sort of." She slipped her sneakers back on.

Howard nodded. They were silent for a few seconds, then he stretched his arm out and made a sweeping gesture across the valley in front of them. "This was one of the first landscapes I painted. It was terrible. Sometime I'm going to come back and re-paint it now that I have a better understanding of lines and colors."

"Are all of your paintings landscapes?" Laurette asked.

"No." He smiled and pushed his hands into the pockets of his jeans. "But I'm not going to tell you what else I paint. You'll have to come over and see for yourself."

She smiled guiltily. "I've been meaning to."

They stood for several more minutes talking, letting the sun warm their faces and the wind drift through their hair. Laurette was just getting ready to start back when Howard nodded toward the creek.

"Isn't that your grandfather down there?"

It was, unfortunately. Laurette's spirits sank as she saw that Grandfather held a full canning jar clasped to his breast.

"What's he carrying?" Howard was puzzled.

"Probably spring water. He has a thing about drinking fresh spring water," she lied.

Howard watched her a moment before his face melted into a smile. "I don't mean to argue, but I think it's white lightning."

She bit her lower lip and kicked at the grass with the toe of her shoe.

At that he threw back his head and laughed. "Your secret is safe with me. I'm not going to tell anyone."

Relief rushed through her and she flashed a grateful smile. "Thanks, Howard."

Grandfather had crossed the creek and started up the hill toward them. "Hello there," he called as unabashedly as if he were carrying a Bible instead of a bottle.

"Hello, Mr. Harrison," Howard said.

"Hi, Grandfather."

By the time he reached them he was panting for breath. "Lovely day for a stroll, ain't it?"

Howard agreed. Laurette merely looked reprovingly at her grandfather.

"I found a bottle of this down by the creek." He held the jar aloft. "I suppose it's spring water, reckon?"

Honestly, what nerve! Laurette shook her head at his insouciance. "Howard thinks it's moonshine," she said baldly.

Grandfather squinted at the contents of the bottle in surprise. "Might be. Hadn't thought of that. I'm not averse to drinking a little 'shine," he added, and went on. "Took up drinking during Prohibition. I didn't have much of a taste for it at the time, but I hated being told what to do, so I kept after it until I developed a taste."

Laurette and Howard exchanged amused glances. "I'm sure you did, Grandfather. That sounds just like you." Affectionately she put her hand on his arm. "We ought to be getting back to the house, don't you think?"

"Good idea." He took his leave of Howard with a

friendly nod and he and Laurette walked up the hill together.

Her thoughts had been temporarily diverted from Jeff, but they returned to him as she and Grandfather threaded around the blackberry bushes. Jeff was making it difficult to keep their relationship platonic when he brought her candy and practiced his charm on her. Again she felt resentment stir. Why couldn't he simply accept the boundaries she had set up and continue to be her friend? She needed a friend far more than she needed a lover right now.

That thought was still on her mind the next morning when Laurette reached the police station door. She was just reaching for the handle when Burris called to her from across the street.

"Well, if it isn't Nancy Drew."

Groaning inwardly, she waited for him to reach her. Belinda had phoned her last night to tell her Stockwell had not seen anything suspicious at the old house. Laurette had resigned herself to the fact that the officers were going to rib her for making a melodrama out of the whole situation.

The squat husky man ambled over to her. "I hear you and Belinda are ready for your detectives' badges."

She gave him a good-humored smile.

"Is that right?" He laughed derisively.

Burris was beginning to get her goat, but Laurette wasn't going to let him see that. "We gave it a shot, but we could never do as good a job as you," she said pleasantly.

118

"Damned right you couldn't."

Her smile was fading rapidly, and if she didn't leave soon she was going to say something she'd regret. "I've got to run, Burris. 'Bye."

She swung into the station feeling annoyed. A quick glance around revealed that Jeff was the only one inside. At the sight of his smile her irritation escalated. Darn Jeff, why did he have to keep undermining her defenses with his compelling smile?

"Hi," she mumbled on her way across to the computer.

"Good morning." Still smiling, he crossed to her desk and pulled up a chair. After turning it around to straddle it, he hooked his arms over the back. "Stockwell tells me you and Belinda were doing some investigating out on West Lane yesterday."

Laurette shrugged indifferently. "We were out there." She kept her chin lifted and her eyes averted.

"He said he didn't find anything unusual."

Again she shrugged and continued to look away from him.

After a moment's pause Jeff asked, "Is something wrong, Etty?"

She faced him squarely. "Not exactly wrong, but I don't see why everyone's making a joke out of this. There could have been something seriously wrong out there. What if there'd been a body in the basement?" she challenged. "Would you still be joking around?"

As he stared at her she saw a light of understanding flicker in his brown eyes. Standing abruptly, he spun the chair around. "I see you're not in the best of spirits. I'll just wander back to my desk and get to work."

It could have ended right there. It should have ended right there, but Laurette was stirred up now and was perversely reluctant to let him leave. "Is that how you handle every situation—by walking away?"

He stared at her through chilly brown eyes. "What is the matter with you today? I was only teasing about the old house. Can't you take a joke?"

"Only if it's funny," she snapped.

"Then I apologize for offending you." But by the clipped way he said the words she knew he wasn't sorry.

"It's because average citizens don't get involved in fighting crime that there's so much of it," she said. "So it seems a little self-defeating for you to poke fun at Belinda and me for investigating a suspicious situation when there wasn't a policeman around to do it."

"I *said* I was sorry."

"You sure didn't sound like you meant it!"

He whirled around and started back for his desk.

"There you go again—running away." It was an outlandish accusation, based on nothing. But the conflicting emotions that Jeff inspired in her had her confused and feeling cornered and she couldn't stop herself from lashing out at him.

Wheeling to face her, he said very deliberately, "I'm not the one who ran away from a job in California, not to mention a husband. I'd say you could look closer to home if you want to criticize someone for failing to face up to situations."

120

Maybe she'd had that one coming, but at the moment Laurette wasn't thinking that clearly, and wasn't in a mood to be fair. "You don't know anything about my job or my marriage. But since you've brought it up, I'll tell you what the problem was. Stan was obsessed with his job and he was positive he was far too important for the company to survive without him. You're the same way about your work. You think this whole place would fall apart without you."

His eyes narrowed and he aimed his index finger at her like a loaded gun. "Look—"

Just then the door opened and Walley slouched in. He stared from one to the other. "Am I interrupting something?" he asked with more insight than he'd shown since Laurette had met him.

"Nothing at all!" She swung around to the computer.

Jeff transferred his angry glare to Walley. "I want to talk to you, Walley," he said fiercely.

"Yeah, sure. First I've got to—"

"Now!"

The silence in the room positively crackled with electricity. Laurette slid a look at Jeff. He was standing in the center of the room, his brows lowered, his mouth as taut as if it were holding straight pins in it. His arms were folded implacably across his chest.

Suddenly the fire went out of Laurette and she sank lower in the chair, wanting to slide out of sight. What had possessed her to provoke a fight with Jeff? Yes, Burris had annoyed her, but the real reason she had struck out at Jeff was that he was making her feel things she didn't want to feel and she felt helpless in the face of those emotions.

"Well, it's going to have to wait a minute, because I have to go to the men's room," Walley said bluntly. He marched off in that direction and Jeff leveled cold eyes back to her.

Fortunately the outside door opened again and Belinda came in, smiling at Jeff.

"Hi. Did Laurette tell you about our exploits yesterday?"

He shot Laurette a cold look. "Not in any detail."

The dark-haired woman, unaware of any undercurrents, continued blithely. "We were quite a pair, let me assure you. The minute we saw footprints in that house we clipped off back to the car like a couple of jackrabbits." She giggled at the memory.

Jeff's face relaxed into something resembling a smile. "Laurette neglected to tell me that in her lengthy account."

Belinda chuckled. "She's being modest."

Laurette watched it all with a growing sense of defeat. It was bad enough for her to have acted like a shrew. But the fact that Belinda was willing to tease and be teased with such charming good humor made Laurette look even worse.

Jeff was smiling at Belinda now; the eyes that had been cold and unyielding to her were now brimming with mirth.

She liked Belinda and she didn't want to be jealous of her, but she had little control over her feelings just now. When Jeff laughed at Belinda's humorous description of their flight to the car, her control slipped even further.

Walley reappeared, shuffling sullenly back into the room. "You wanted to talk to me?"

"In a minute," Jeff said absently.

Walley looked relieved.

"Why don't you take Laurette and me to coffee and we'll tell you the whole story?" Belinda suggested gaily.

Laurette tensed. She was too embarrassed over having blasted into Jeff without provocation to manage a conversation right now. "You two go ahead. I'm too busy." To prove it, she began randomly pushing buttons on the computer.

Belinda hesitated. "You're sure?"

Jeff said nothing.

"Positive." Laurette continued working as she talked. "I'm in the middle of something I can't leave."

But the moment the door closed behind Jeff and Belinda, she turned the machine off and propped her elbows against the terminal. If they gave out awards for irrational behavior, she was first in line.

CHAPTER EIGHT

Jeff wasn't at the station the next morning when Laurette arrived, and she breathed a sigh of relief. She wasn't ready yet to face him after having made such a fool of herself yesterday. She would have to apologize to him, of course.

She had lain awake half the night last night trying to come to terms with her feelings. She never had, but she did realize it was wrong to blame Jeff because she was attracted to him.

Laurette was pouring herself a cup of coffee when Jeff came in. He looked at her warily. With a nod of greeting she turned back to filling her cup and tried to recall her rehearsed words of apology. When she turned around again she was face to face with him. Although he wasn't smiling, there was a glitter that might have been humor in his eyes. Laurette wasn't sure what his mood was.

"Would you like some coffee?" she asked with tentative politeness.

He lounged against a nearby desk and buffed a brass button on his uniform against his shirt sleeve.

"That depends on whether you intend to hand it to me or throw it at me." He was grinning broadly now.

The corners of her mouth rose in a faint answering smile. "I understand why you're wary of me. I guess I did fly off the handle yesterday. I'm sorry." It was hard to meet his direct gaze, so she settled for looking at a spot just over his right shoulder.

Jeff glanced behind him, then back at her. "Are you talking to me?" he asked innocently.

She bit her lower lip. "You know I am."

"Then look at me."

Slowly she obeyed and found herself gazing into a pair of deep brown eyes. "I—I want to apologize," she began hesitantly. "I—"

"Forget it. We both said things we didn't mean and we're both sorry."

"Yes," she murmured. Jeff had straightened and moved a step toward her so that they were now standing close.

He smiled. "Now that we've got that settled, I suppose it's safe to accept that coffee."

She was glad to have an excuse to have something to do with her hands.

"So how's your grandfather?" he asked easily as he accepted a fresh cup and handed hers back to her.

Laurette took a long, slow sip. As long as Jeff had brought up the subject, why not tell him exactly how her grandfather was, right down to the fact that he was making moonshine? Surely if she confided in him, Jeff would momentarily forget his position as chief of police and help her as a friend.

Clearing her throat, she began leading into the subject. "Well, the truth is——"

With the worst of all timing the telephone rang. Jeff gave a smile and shrug of resignation and picked up the receiver. "Yeah, Burris, what is it?"

Laurette couldn't hear the conversation on the other end, but she saw a frown shadow his features. Then he began shaking his head. "No, we're not going to do that, Burris. If the mayor's son was in on the vandalism, then he gets hauled in with the other four kids. We're not giving anybody special treatment just because of who they are."

There was another silence during which Burris seemed to be arguing.

Jeff was more adamant now. "I don't care if his father is the President and his mother is the Queen of England. That's not the way this town is being run. The law is the law and anyone who breaks it can expect the same treatment."

She half choked on her coffee. Well, that certainly answered her question! It was lucky for her the phone had rung before she'd made her confession.

"Right. I'll see you later." Jeff hung up and turned back to her. His voice changed from brusque to silky, almost seductive. "Now then, what were you saying, Etty?"

She looked around for an escape. "Um, I don't remember." Flashing a dazzling smile, she started to edge past him. "Well, I'd better get back to work."

Jeff caught hold of her arm. "You were talking about your grandfather," he reminded her.

She managed to look blank. "Was I?"

"Yes." Jeff's hand tightened around her arm and he watched her narrowly. "Are you having problems with him? You can tell me if you are, Etty."

The soft persuasiveness of Jeff's words made her yearn to confide in him. But his words to Burris still rang in her ear. Jeff wasn't going to be lenient with anyone who broke the law, including her grandfather. As badly as she wanted Grandfather out of the moonshine business, she didn't want him to go to jail!

Lowering her lashes, she stared down at a black scuff mark on the tile floor, tracing it back and forth with her toe. "No problems. Grandfather and I are getting along just fine."

Jeff put his index finger beneath her chin and tilted her face upward until she was again looking at him. "A lot of older people get senile, Etty. It's nothing to be ashamed about."

Laurette began to breathe again, relieved at his misunderstanding.

"I'm sure your being here is good for him," Jeff continued.

"I hope so." She and Jeff were within inches of each other. She could see the tiny lines around his eyes that crinkled when he smiled, and smell the pleasant musk scent of his aftershave. The air between them was charged with a tension that sent excitement cascading down her spine.

"Have dinner with me tonight, Etty."

His invitation caught her off guard and her instant reaction was to say yes. After all, it was only dinner. How passionate could things possibly get in a public restaurant? Besides, she thought to herself with a small smile, friends did have dinner together.

Jeff touched her hair, softly brushing back an errant curl. "Let's make it seven thirty."

"I haven't said I would," she protested weakly.

"You haven't said you wouldn't." He was playing with another curl now and his fingers grazed her ear. She felt warm feelings spring to life. "I like your hair," he murmured. "It's so soft and shiny."

She felt the delightfully rough texture of his hand as it began gliding down the back of her neck. Tremors of pleasure rippled through her. She was defeated and she knew it, but she wasn't even upset about losing the battle. In fact, she was already looking forward to tonight.

"Seven thirty sounds fine," she breathed.

He smiled a slow, easy smile. "Good. I'll pick you up then."

At five o'clock Laurette whisked out of the office and back to her grandfather's house. After brushing her hair into carefree curls and dressing in a teal silk blouse and skirt, she stepped into the living room. Grandfather looked up from his paper, peering at her through the top half of his bifocals.

She crossed the room and kissed him on the forehead. "Hi, Grandfather. Did you have a nice day?"

" 'Twas awright," he grunted.

"That's good," she said gaily. It would have taken more than Grandfather's grumpiness to burst her bubble of happy anticipation. Now that she had agreed to have dinner with Jeff, she refused to dwell on any reasons why she shouldn't go.

"You got some mail. From the phone company," he added ominously. He'd disapproved of having another phone put in, warning her against doing business with "those shysters." Now he watched her with a gratified I-told-you-so expression as she picked up the letter from the table by the door.

"It's probably some form letter about the rates," she said as she tore the letter open with an air of unconcern. Her smile faded as she skimmed the letter. It informed her she would have to put down a deposit to cover her large number of long distance calls to New York.

Indignantly she reread the letter. "What long distance calls to New York?" she demanded aloud.

"I *knew* you'd have trouble with that bunch. Didn't I tell you?" Grandfather looked grimly pleased at having his prediction come true.

"I haven't made any long distance calls to New York," she insisted.

He ran spindly fingers through his white hair, making it stand up on end. "Don't pay 'em a cent!"

"I certainly don't intend to pay for any calls I haven't made."

"That's the spirit!" Grandfather was obviously relishing the upcoming fight. "Show 'em what you're made of."

Her grandfather was only agitating her more, Laurette realized, and that wouldn't get her anywhere. Drawing in a deep breath, she made an effort to recover her calm. "Obviously there's been a mistake. I'll simply go to the phone company and explain that."

"Hah! Don't expect 'em to listen. Bunch of crooks. *That's* who the police ought to be out chasing instead of sitting around with their feet on their desks like they do."

A knock on the door prevented Laurette from replying. Since the front door was open against the summer heat, she could see Jeff standing outside the screen door. Naturally he'd heard Grandfather's crack about the police.

"Somebody's at the door," Grandfather said unnecessarily.

"Yes, I'll get it." What a wonderful beginning to the evening, Laurette thought wryly. With her smile firmly in place, she crossed to the door and opened it. "Hello, Jeff. Come in."

When he stepped inside, Laurette saw he was dressed smartly in a pair of brown duck trousers and a beige cotton shirt. His smile was warm.

"Hello, Mr. Harrison," Jeff said formally.

Grandfather looked him over, then nodded abruptly. " 'Lo."

Her grandfather was not going to put himself out to be cordial, Laurette realized, so the sooner they got out of here, the better. Scooping up her purse, she announced, "I'm ready. Don't wait up for me, Grandfather."

"I wasn't goin' to." He ducked back behind the paper.

Jeff was privately amused by the old man's contrariness, but Laurette seemed flustered by it, so he tactfully said nothing. When he slid in behind the wheel of his car she was still settling herself on the passenger side, giving much attention to smoothing her skirt.

"Where are we going to eat?" she asked.

"My place."

She jerked her head around to face him. "I thought we'd go to a restaurant."

He shot her a devilish grin. "What's the matter? Are you afraid to try my cooking?"

"No. I—it's not that; it's just that I wasn't expecting to go to your house. . . ." Her words trailed off vaguely, and she began to fidget with her hands.

"Well, we *are* going to my house," he said stoutly and started the car. "I haven't slaved over a hot stove all day for nothing. I expect some appreciation for all my hard work."

"I'm sure it'll be very good," she murmured, but she still sounded hesitant.

Jeff backed out of the driveway and started toward his house. He had come prepared to talk down any objections she had about going to his house for dinner. Tonight he wanted to be alone with her. It was high time they came to a better understanding of each other. This "friendship" she wanted to lock them into was a lot of bull. He wanted to be much more than a friend to her, and judging from what he'd seen, so did she.

While he didn't claim to be the world's foremost authority on women, he did know when a woman was interested in him in ways that were totally female. And that was exactly the interest Laurette had in him, whether she wanted to admit it or not.

131

Minutes later he pulled up in front of his house, a small bungalow that had been built in the early twenties and sat in middle of a block of similar houses.

"Here we are." He opened her door and cupped a hand on the small of her back as they walked toward the house. When they reached the front door he opened the door and stepped back to allow her to enter. As he followed her in he glanced around the living room. It was clean although sparsely furnished, and linoleum rather than a rug covered the floor. The furniture consisted of an end table, two straight-back chairs and a navy cut-velvet divan that was vintage fifties. The place would never make *House Beautiful,* but he considered it adequate for his needs. He wondered what she thought of it.

Laurette stood stiffly beside the door, as if she hadn't quite decided whether to run or to stay. Jeff wanted to laugh at her timidity, but managed to maintain an impassive expression.

"How long have you lived here?" she asked.

"Two years. It was pretty run down when I bought it," he added. "I've mostly worked on repairing structural problems and haven't done much decorating." Nothing like stating the obvious, he thought with inner amusement.

Laurette stepped away from the door and studied the room with great interest. "It has possibilities." She touched a richly carved trim board at the side of the fireplace. "Nice wood trim. A print wallpaper would look very pretty in here."

He watched her eyes move on to the windows and knew that she was mentally selecting drapes to replace the plastic shades. While she looked at the windows he looked at her. She was a study in supple, unconscious grace as she moved to the center of the room, put a hand on the swell of her hip, and frowned thoughtfully. As he watched Laurette he was tempted to forget the meal entirely and sweep her off her feet, carry her into the meagerly furnished bedroom, and let her turn her attention to *that* for a while.

Instead, he headed through the living room toward the Pullman-style kitchen. "Come on back and help make the salad."

She sighed elaborately but followed. "I thought I was the guest."

For an answer he handed her a chef's apron with the word SLAVE printed across the front. The one he tied around himself with excessive fastidiousness bore the word MASTER.

Laughing, she pushed her apron back toward him. "Oh, no. I'm not wearing *this.*"

He shrugged. "All my women wear that apron . . . or they wear nothing at all."

Giggling, she lifted her eyebrows archly. "Those are my only choices?"

"That's right. I have no objections to the latter," he added hopefully.

Laurette took the apron and tied it around herself —wrong side out so that the Slave lettering was concealed. She tossed him a smug smile and began rolling up the sleeves of her blouse. "Where's the lettuce?"

Ten minutes later the meal was on the kitchen

table. In addition to the salad, they had spaghetti and garlic bread.

She took her place across from him at the Formica table and tasted the spaghetti. "Mmmm. The sauce is delicious."

"Thank you," he said modestly. "I made it from scratch."

"You did not! I saw the empty jar in the wastebasket." Her eyes sparkled with amusement.

He liked her eyes when they were like that. They brought out the woman in her and spoke of a come-to-bed sensuality. At other times she could look like an enchanting girl, with her little turned-up nose and the light freckles sprinkled across her cheeks. He found her alluring both ways.

Laurette aimed her fork at him and fought back a laugh. "Admit it. You didn't make the sauce."

He was piously affronted. "I never thought that you would question my word—"

"Admit it!" She was laughing now, revealing even white teeth and the flirtatious dimple.

The more he saw of her, the more the need within him grew for her. She was very special to him. She could be warm and understanding, but he was sure she could also be tough if the situation called for it. Most of all, he trusted her in a way that he trusted few other people. He wished that she were ready to trust him, but he knew she still intended to keep anything serious from developing between them. He meant to do everything he could tonight to kill those reservations.

* * *

After dinner Laurette helped Jeff clear the dishes. He washed; she dried. After she put the last dish away in the cupboard, she began taking off her apron.

"Let me help," he said.

She turned around to allow him to untie the sash, but he didn't. Instead, his arms encircled her waist and he drew her back against him. She went willingly. It had been a pleasant evening. Beneath their light banter she had detected a note of sensuality. More than once she had looked up to see his eyes resting steadily on her, making her feel more sure of his desire than if he'd told her outright that he wanted her in his bed.

He wrapped his arms more tightly around her and dropped a kiss on her cheek, then on her neck. Laurette closed her eyes and leaned more fully against him. He had rolled up his shirt sleeves earlier and she could feel the sinewy strength of his arms across her midsection. Arching her neck further back against him, she smiled at the light, feathery touch of his kiss.

Then he was turning her toward him. She opened her eyes and looked down at the hair clinging damply to his arms, then up into his cocoa brown eyes. The banter they had shared at the table had been left behind. He looked very solemn and wistful now, and she knew he was waiting for a sign from her before he became too insistent.

Was this the right thing to do? she wondered, and knew the answer didn't matter because, right or wrong, she'd already made her choice. She could read his need for her in the depths of his eyes and she needed him just as much. Slipping her hands up to his neck, she locked them together in his brown hair and brought her mouth up to his.

Their lips met first in tentative wonder, then settled more fully together. She felt the soft cushion of his lower lip move against her mouth, felt him teasing her lips apart, and then they were united in a consuming kiss. His tongue flitted inside her mouth and set aflame sensations that raced up and down her body. Her fingers moved from his hair to his neck, then strayed over to his ear. She felt him quiver with desire when they dallied there. Each kiss became more searching and wrenching than the one before.

His hands moved down her sides, stopping at her hips to draw her closer against him, then moved up to her breasts and wandered over them. She felt her heartbeat move to three-quarter time, and her breathing became irregular. When his lips left hers and nestled in her ear, her heartbeat jumped altogether.

He whispered into her ear—soft, unintelligible words that made her feel very willing while he laced his fingers through her hair and threaded kisses along her neck. She grew even more willing.

In one movement he gathered her up into his arms and carried her out of the kitchen and through the dusk-filled house to the bedroom. There he set her on her feet and began to undress her. Her lids fell closed and she let her head fall back, luxuriating in the erotic feeling of his hands dancing over her. He stopped now and then to kiss her shoulder or wrist before resuming his task of removing her clothes with loving patience. When her skirt and blouse and underclothes finally rested in a dainty heap on the bare floor, he picked her up and put her on the bed.

She slid between the crisp, fresh sheets and watched him move about in the dark room, hearing the soft thumps of his own clothes hitting the floor. Then he stole into bed beside her.

His arms came around her with as much urgency as if they had been separated for many months rather than a few moments. She appreciated his fervor, for she felt it too. And the feeling was growing even stronger. Everything about him excited her. The light hair of his legs was a delicious contrast to her smooth ones, and his raw strength contrasted with her own feminine softness. Wreathing her arms around his neck, she lost herself in his drugging kisses.

She felt his masculine desire unfold to life against her and was inordinately pleased to be the source of that desire. While she continued to swim in the honey of his kisses, she let her hands roam at will over the landscape of his body. The tips of her fingers grazed over hard arm muscles that were cloaked with satiny skin, then moved down to the hair on his chest and the bare expanse of skin on his stomach.

At the same time his hands were following the curves and contours of her own body in a way that made her catch her breath. They dallied in the warm and sensitive avenue between the swell of her breasts before stealing up to capture the pink aureole between thumb and forefinger and tug gently. His mouth swept away from hers and grazed a path downward to replace his hands. When his lips settled on the tips of her breasts, she felt a hot rush of pleasure.

By the time they finally linked in the ultimate embrace, her body was alive with desire for him. Her soft murmurs became whimpers of joy as he arched himself against her and drew them even closer together. What began as a gentle rocking motion became steadily more urgent until she was caught in the wild spell of passion. She unconsciously raked her hands over his back, wanting to attach herself more firmly to the source of her ecstasy as they soared into space together. She heard faint cries of bliss that she only vaguely recognized as her own.

CHAPTER NINE

Afterward Laurette cuddled against Jeff and drifted into a languid drowsiness. He had been all the right things at all the right times—thoughtful, demanding, giving. And his attention to her hadn't ended with their lovemaking. Even now he continued to hold her, occasionally stroking his hand along her bare back or whispering a word of tenderness.

Covers rustling, she crept closer into the soft cave of his arms and smiled her contentment. For several moments they lay in peaceful silence.

All the effort she had expended to keep this from happening had not only been wasted, it had been foolish. What had she been afraid of anyway? Jeff was everything Stan had not been. The rare nights when she and Stan had made love had disturbed rather than reassured her. He had seemed so detached, as if his mind were still wrestling with a computer problem while his body went through the motions. But it hadn't been that way with Jeff. She had had his full attention and she knew he had lost himself in her as completely as she had lost herself in him.

A sliver of doubt wedged itself between her and Jeff, and Laurette shifted restlessly on the bed. All right, so she and Jeff had made love and it had been a supremely rewarding experience. But what now? Where was their relationship going to go from here? After all, Jeff intended to stay in Locust Grove the rest of his life, and she did not.

She felt him brush his fingers gently through her hair and drop a kiss on her neck. In that moment her doubts were forgotten. The future didn't need to be decided tonight, she rationalized. What was important was that she and Jeff had shared something exquisite and it was enough for now to savor the delicious afterglow.

The shrill ring of the telephone pierced the silence in the room.

Still keeping an arm around her, Jeff leaned over and picked up the receiver. "Yeah?" he said languidly. Instantly his words became sharp. "When? Yes, I'll be right down." He hung up the phone and threw back the covers. "I've got to go."

One moment Laurette's head was resting at the juncture of Jeff's neck and the next she was lying on a cool sheet in an empty bed. She felt like a discarded toy after a child's hectic Christmas. "Where are you going?" she asked in a stricken voice.

"To the station. There's a problem."

She heard the rustling of clothing and lifted herself onto one elbow. "But there are men on duty. Can't they handle this?"

"No." He flipped on a light and she saw that he was already fully dressed. Reaching toward the bedside table, he pulled a drawer open and drew out a gun. "You stay here," he directed absently. "I'll take you home when I get back."

That was it. Without another word he left the house, turning the bedroom light out as he went. Laurette fell back in the solitary bed and felt the first tears welling up in her eyes. How could he do this to her? How could he leave her like this?

She had given herself to him without reservation. Surely he must know how much it would hurt her to be abandoned like this so soon after their lovemaking. But clearly Jeff neither understood nor cared to understand about her needs. By leaving to go to the station he'd made it plain where his priorities lay.

Laurette had to get away; she could no longer remain in this house. Brushing away a fresh crop of tears, she climbed out of the bed and began searching for her clothes in the dark room. She couldn't bear to turn the light on and see the disheveled bed where only minutes before she and Jeff had made love.

If only the phone hadn't rung . . . She bit her lower lip to steady it. The phone *had* rung and now he was gone. But she wasn't going to play second fiddle to a job for any man again. Surely there were other men on the force who could have handled whatever had come up tonight, yet Jeff had gone tearing out to take care of it himself—without giving her a second thought.

Well, let him go, but she darn sure wasn't going to be waiting when he returned. She was down on one knee searching for a shoe when a freezing thought hit her. What if Jeff didn't come back? After all, his was a dangerous line of work and every time he went out on a call there was a chance he wouldn't come back.

The word *dangerous* had not truly registered with her until this minute. Yes, she knew Jeff had been shot and injured, but that had been in Memphis, and she had assumed he was safe in Locust Grove. But was he? Her spirits sank as she recalled Jeff opening the drawer and pulling out a gun. If there had been no need for one, he surely wouldn't have taken it. With more strength than she knew she possessed she finished dressing, found her way out into the living room, and turned on the light. It was bad enough to be left in an empty house, but worrying if something might happen to Jeff was more than she could endure. She had to get out of here.

Looping her purse over her shoulder, she walked out the door and down the steps into the dark summer night. Her heels clicked loudly on the deserted streets, but she was too engulfed in her feelings of hurt and betrayal to worry much about the dangers that might lurk in the dark, even in Locust Grove. She walked into the pitch blackness beneath a large tree without a second thought.

Fifteen minutes later she pushed the screen door to her grandfather's house open and stepped inside. Grandfather was snoring in the overstuffed chair. She locked the front door as quietly as possible and tiptoed across the room toward the stairs. The snoring stopped.

"No need for creepin' around," came a fuzzy voice from the depths of the chair.

Laurette turned back to him. "I'm sorry I woke you, Grandfather."

"I wasn't asleep," he proclaimed testily, and dragged out his pocketwatch out to squint at it. Then he glowered at her. "Do you know what time it is, young lady?"

"Not exactly."

"It's almost two! What in the Sam Hill kind of time is that for a respectable fella to be bringing a gal home?"

She busied herself finger-combing her hair. Her grandfather would have expired on the spot if he'd realized she'd walked home by herself. And if he'd known some of the other things that had happened tonight he'd really raise his voice. "We, uh, we lost track of time," she mumbled.

"In my day when a man was seein' a woman he . . ."

In spite of the fact that she wanted desperately to be alone and finish the cry she had started at Jeff's house, Laurette listened stoically to her grandfather's lecture. As soon as he was finished, however, she said, "You look awfully tired. Maybe we should go up to bed and talk about this in the morning. Besides," she added over her shoulder, "I'm not going to be seeing Jeff again. That's all over."

Grandfather heaved himself out of the chair. "I've heard that before." He continued to mutter to himself as he crept up the stairs after her.

Laurette held up very well until she was lying in bed in her girlish cotton nightgown. Then she could control the tears no longer.

143

* * *

Locust Grove had been a relatively tame town for the past eight months, but all hell had broken loose tonight. From the moment Jeff had received Burris's excited phone call, things had been hopping. He arrived at the station to find a shaken Stockwell and an ashen Burris huddled together over cigarettes and coffee.

"What happened?" Jeff demanded.

Stockwell spoke first. "We'd just come on duty—Burris and I—when two men came in wearing ski masks and carrying submachine guns." He pressed his fingers to his temple and paused to take a shaky draw on his cigarette. "I've never had one of those things pointed at me before, and let me tell you I didn't much like the feeling."

"Yeah," Burris agreed. He was hunched in a corner chair, his stubby fingers clamped together and dangling between his legs while his eyes moved from the door to the windows, as if he were awaiting the second wave of an attack.

"Then what happened?" Jeff asked calmly. He was determined not to let it show, but he felt unnerved himself. It wasn't often that two policemen were held at gunpoint in a police station.

Stockwell took up the story. "Then one of them—the big one—rifled around through the desk drawers like he was looking for something."

"The little one held the gun on us," Burris said faintly.

Jeff looked around at the dozen desk drawers still

144

hanging open. "Did they find what they were looking for?"

Burris nodded. "Yeah. The big guy took a key and went out the back door. I think it was the key to the stolen property room."

"And what did the other man do?" Jeff asked.

"He took our wallets and tied us up." Stockwell spoke in a low voice; the memory of the incident was clearly painful.

Jeff sympathized with the men. He knew how humiliating it would be for any good policeman to be at the mercy of a criminal.

Stockwell ground out his cigarette and scowled down at the floor. "I shouldn't have let him tie us up. I could have overpowered that runt and taken his gun"

Jeff shook his head. "You did the right thing. There's no reason for any tombstone heroism against an armed man. All that would have gotten you is a hero's funeral."

"Anyway," Burris continued in an unsteady voice, "he didn't tie us up too well and it didn't take long to get untied. By that time, though, they were both gone."

"But you heard their vehicle pull out?" Jeff asked quickly.

"Yes. It was parked out back."

"What did it sound like?"

"A car," Stockwell said.

"A van," Burris answered.

"Which way was it headed?"

"West," Burris said at the same time that Stockwell replied, "Due east."

Great, Jeff thought dryly, stifling his exasperation. Not only did he not have a license number, he didn't even have a direction to begin looking in. "You two get out on the streets and find somebody who saw that vehicle. Try Cal's Pool Hall first. There might have been some high school kids hanging around out front. I'm going to do some dusting for prints." He didn't have much hope of differentiating among the other prints that were bound to be all over the desks and the back door, but he'd give it a try. "I'll check the stolen property room and see if I can determine what they took." Now *that* was going to be a nightmare task. On second thought, he'd call Walley and let him handle that since Walley was responsible for the chaos the place was in.

After Burris and Stockwell left, Jeff went out the back door, taking care not to touch the knob and smear any fingerprints that might be on it. He crossed the alley into the stolen property room and found the door gaping wide open.

He had worked enough robberies to recognize this case had all the earmarks of something well thought out in advance. It might take time to solve, and he'd probably be up all night getting started on it.

With a sudden stab of guilt he remembered that Laurette was waiting back at his house. Closing the door of the stolen property room, he crossed the alley back to the station. The timing of this robbery couldn't have been worse. It didn't take much imagination to figure how Laurette must have felt when

146

he'd scrambled out of the house and disappeared so shortly after they'd made love.

But he had a job to do, he defended himself. Surely she realized that. She'd also understand if he called and told her he wouldn't be back for several hours. Inside the station he picked up the phone and dialed his home number. The phone at his house rang several times, but no one answered.

Concerned, he hung up and tried again. Still no answer. He was beginning to worry. What reason could there be for her not answering the phone? It sat right there by the bed. Even if she'd gone back to sleep the ring was so loud it was bound to wake her. Was something *wrong?*

Worry grabbed at him, tempting him to slam down the receiver and rush back to his house to make sure she was safe.

"Let's not lose our cool, Murray," he cautioned himself aloud.

There must be a logical explanation. Laurette might have gone back to her grandfather's house. That didn't seem likely because she had no transportation, but before he got carried away worrying, he'd better call the old man's house and check. After getting the number from the operator he dialed and waited impatiently.

The phone rang six times before a sleepy, familiar voice came on the line. "Hello."

His tight muscles uncoiled. Thank God she was safe! Almost immediately his relief turned to anger. What in thunder was she doing at her grandfather's? He had left her at his house. "Laurette?" he snapped.

147

"Yes."

"It's Jeff." He was fighting to bring his anger under control, but having little luck. He had told her to wait for him, but she must have left the house the instant he was gone or she couldn't have made it back to her grandfather's already. And been asleep to boot! "How did you get home?"

"I walked."

"You walked!" With two maniacs toting machine guns loose! "What in the hell kind of childish stunt was that?" he shouted.

For answer she slammed the receiver down in his ear.

Laurette didn't sleep well that night. After Jeff's call she had lain awake tallying up all the things she wished she'd said to him. How dare he be angry with her for leaving his house! *He* was the one who had walked out on her over what was probably some petty bit of police business. In a way her anger was a blessing, for it kept her feelings of rejection and pain at bay. Gradually, however, the anger deserted her and she was left facing a hurt so searing it scorched her heart.

The next morning, as she stood in the bathroom surveying the dark hollows beneath her eyes, she debated whether or not to go in to work at all. Why didn't she just quit? She wasn't getting rich from the job, and if she continued, it was going to mean more contact with Jeff. And she didn't want that.

Even as she blamed him for her unhappiness, however, she knew part of her anger was really directed toward herself. When was she going to learn to take control of her own life? She'd come into town like a wounded puppy fresh from a good kicking. Although she'd made a few token protests against becoming involved, *she* was the one responsible for letting her feelings for Jeff get out of hand. She'd begun by letting him talk her into coming to work for him, and last night she'd let him take her to his house for dinner when she should have known where that would lead.

Well, from now on she was steering the ship. And the first thing she was going to do was to get her future in perspective. She'd begin by finding an employment counselor—there must be one in Knoxville —getting a job, and beginning her new life.

Satisfied with that decision, Laurette brushed her honey blond hair with new resolve. She wasn't going to quit. She wouldn't give Jeff the satisfaction of thinking she was afraid to face him.

Momentarily, however, she faltered in her resolve. Last night had been very special, an intimacy beyond intimacy. Her hunger for Jeff had been more than sexual, and he had satisfied her needs in ways so achingly tender that the memory brought a lump to her throat. She remembered his soft words of love, the trembling of his hands on her body as if he were overwhelmed by the gift she was making of herself. She remembered the reassuring way he had held her afterward. All those things had made their union more than two bodies coming together, sweetening it with the nectar of romance.

Was she being unreasonable to have expected Jeff

to stay with her when he had been called by duty? He probably hadn't wanted to leave that bed any more than she had wanted him to. With the right words of apology he might have induced her to forgive him. That thought brought Laurette back to earth with a thud, and her anger steamrolled over her softening emotions. Jeff had sounded anything but sweet and apologetic when he had called her last night.

Rising, Laurette strode from the room. Jeff had had no right to bark at her over the phone. He hadn't even *asked* her to wait for him at his house, he had ordered her to. And being told what to do always had a way of making Laurette feel contrary, undoubtably a trait she had inherited from her grandfather. With her head held high she marched down the stairs to the kitchen.

Grandfather was standing by the refrigerator when she walked in. "There you are," he greeted her.

"Good morning." She wasn't angry with him, but the words still came out clipped.

She felt his eyes following her around the room as she took a bowl and a box of cereal out of the cupboard and fished a spoon out of the silverware drawer.

"What's the matter with you today?" he demanded. "You've got a face that would curdle milk."

"I'm still a little sleepy, that's all."

Unfortunately that was the wrong thing to say. Grandfather pounced. "No wonder you're bone-tired with the hours you're keepin'. A body can't stay out half the night and expect to be fit for anything the next day."

Laurette nodded. She didn't feel like arguing with him this morning. Wordlessly she poured milk over her cereal and began eating her cornflakes.

Grandfather sat down across from her. "Are you going to talk to those yahoos at the phone company?" he demanded.

In the emotional turmoil of last night, Laurette had forgotten about that. "I guess I will," she said listlessly.

"Tell 'em to come and take the damn thing out!"

Laurette paused with her spoon in midair. Her appetite, what little she'd had to begin with, had deserted her. She put the spoon back into the bowl and carried it to the sink.

"That's all you're going to eat? No wonder you're so tired and puny."

As much as Laurette loved her grandfather, he was not making this day any easier for her. "I'll buy a doughnut later," she said to stifle further argument. " 'Bye."

She stopped at the phone company on the way to work and received a guarantee they would send someone out to test the lines. Ten minutes later she pushed through the police station door and stopped short. She'd never seen so many people in the office.

Jeff was standing by his desk talking to two policemen while the county sheriff, a husky man with broad shoulders, sat at a nearby desk speaking into the telephone. Three other uniformed men conferred over a map. Additional officers were scattered

151

around at other desks. Walley was digging through the file cabinets like a squirrel anxiously trying to find nuts he had buried last fall. Amid the flurry of activity no one noticed her.

She closed the door behind her. Stockwell looked up and nodded. "Good morning. You've missed most of the excitement."

"Oh?" Her eyes went involuntarily to Jeff, who had lifted his head and was staring at her icily. "What happened?" she asked.

Jeff outlined the events with cool briefness and concluded, "We're working with the state police now, trying to apprehend the men."

"I see." Jeff continued to watch her from across the room. She read a challenge in his hands-on-hip stance and in the hard lines of his face, and tilted her own chin upward fractionally in reply. If she had been wrong to blame him for leaving her in the middle of the night, then he had been equally at fault for his harsh words to her on the phone.

Stockwell tugged at Jeff's arm. "It's possible those men didn't leave town by one of the main highways. Maybe they knew the side roads. Of course that would indicate local talent. Walley's pulling the files on all the birds who live around here who've ever done time."

Jeff nodded in reply, but his eyes remained locked with Laurette's in silent combat. Both had accusations to make, but Laurette knew this was neither the time nor the place. In one abrupt movement she turned on her heel and walked over to the computer.

CHAPTER TEN

The office was a hotbed of activity for the rest of the day, making it difficult for Laurette to concentrate on her job. Either someone was leaning over her to get to the boxes of files on the floor near her, or she was pausing to listen to the men discussing an interesting theory about the crime. Reporters filed in and out of the office all day, including ones from the UPI and AP wire services. The phone didn't stop ringing.

Adding to the confusion around her was the inner turbulence of her emotions. Why had she let things go so far between her and Jeff last night? she demanded of herself over and over again. If only she had stopped herself before they'd made love, then they could still be friends. But they had made love and now it was too late to retreat back into a casual friendship. Neither could they continue the passionate relationship that had begun last night.

While she couldn't deny their moment of passion had been exhilarating, the aftermath was even more painful than she had feared. She still felt chilled and empty when she thought of being left alone in Jeff's bedroom. True, now that she knew why he'd left she admitted he'd had no choice but to go. Yet recognizing that fact didn't lessen her sense of desolation. Always, it seemed, she was being left alone and waiting for the man she cared about. It was better that she and Jeff put an end to their relationship now, before she suffered even more.

Perversely, however, Laurette found herself constantly stealing glances at Jeff. It was as if he held a magnetic pull that she was incapable of resisting. Once, when her eyes sought him out, their gazes collided. She maintained a regal expression as she turned away, but beneath the surface a riot of other emotions flowed.

However much she might regret what had happened between her and Jeff last night, it *had* happened. And in its wake was the memory of his touch, the husky need in his voice, and the tender furor of his kisses. She couldn't undo what had been done last night, she told herself, but she had to put the memories aside. That wasn't easy to do when Jeff was in the same room with her, keeping those memories vividly in mind by his sheer presence.

It was impossible for Laurette to get any work done in such a charged atmosphere. By five o'clock she felt like an emotional dishrag and was more than ready to go home. She was just picking up her purse when Jeff stopped beside her desk.

"I think we need to talk," he said. The voices of the other men and the noise of the ringing phone provided them a measure of privacy.

"Oh?" Judging by the tight lines around his mouth and the cold nut-brown depths of his eyes, what Jeff had in mind wasn't a down-on-his-knees apology. Not that she wanted him to apologize. It was far better to end things between them right now. "About what?" she asked with a coolness calculated to hide the turmoil she was feeling.

"Don't play games with me." His voice was low and tense. Unexpectedly he caught her by the arm and propelled her toward the back door. The men in the room were too busy to notice, and Laurette was too embarrassed to make a scene. But she wasn't about to let Jeff get away with hauling her around like that. As soon as they were outside the back door, she yanked her arm away from him.

"Just what do you think you're doing?" she asked indignantly.

"You've been sitting at your desk sulking all day. I think it's about time we have a discussion like two mature adults."

"Fine," she returned sarcastically.

Sighing raggedly, Jeff combed his fingers through his hair. His eyes slowly narrowed as his exasperation galvanized into anger and he crossed his arms over his chest like a forbidding Buddha. "If you're mad because I went off and left you last night, you're being unreasonable. It was my *job* to go. Anyone can understand I didn't have any choice."

"Maybe you did have to go last night," she conceded. "But I can't help thinking any call you'd gotten would have set you springing out of that bed."

"I don't know what the hell you want from me," he fumed.

"I don't want anything from you! Last night was

a mistake, and we should just leave it at that." She kept her chin angled up and her voice cold, but in the back of her mind she knew this was a sham. Her only armor against him was to keep her anger pitched high. To see Jeff's side for even a few minutes would make her soften toward him, to think of last night, to remember his hoarse endearments. . . .

"A mistake," he repeated incredulously. "What the hell do you mean?"

"I mean that we should never have—have gone beyond being friends." She knitted her hands tighter over her purse, but couldn't quite meet his gaze.

"Oh, for heaven's sake!" He expelled a tight breath, narrowed the distance between them in one step, and placed a strong hand around her arm. When he spoke again his voice was gentle. "Don't be like this, Etty. You're scared and looking for a reason to run."

"That's n-not true," she said, surprised at the knot in her voice.

"It *is* true, and you know it. Why, I was barely out of my house last night before you went flying home. By the way, you had no business going out by yourself in the middle of the night. It's not safe at the best of times, and it certainly wasn't safe last night with armed men running around. I told you I'd be back."

The warmth of his touch and the quiet logic of his words were undermining her defenses. Laurette forced herself to recall all those nights when another man had assured her he would be home "early" and had not shown up until two or three in the morning—

if at all. "But you didn't get back home last night, did you?" she challenged quietly.

Jeff started to speak, stopped, then spread his hands in a gesture of defeat. "No, I didn't. I couldn't." Tiredly he ran his fingers through his hair. "Look, it's been a long day and our nerves are strained right now. This isn't the time to be making any hasty decisions about our future."

It was on the tip of her tongue to tell him she knew enough about her future to be certain that he wouldn't be in it. But the sag in Jeff's shoulders kept her from speaking. And for the first time she saw the fatigue in his face and the tiny lines etched around his eyes. Jeff was more than tired, she realized with a start, he was in pain. After a sleepless night he was not only exhausted, but his leg must be bothering him as well.

Her coldness toward him melted with the swiftness of a spring thaw. All of a sudden he seemed much more like the young Jeff with the cowlick that couldn't be combed down and the dirt-streaked face. His look of vulnerability brought out her gentle, protective side.

"You're tired; you should go home," she said.

He shook his head and nodded over his shoulder toward the police station. "There's too much work to do here."

"Leave it," she said flatly.

The lines in his face eased slightly, and amusement flirted in his eyes. "You're getting bossy, Etty."

"I most certainly am, and if you've got any sense at all, you'll listen to me. You belong home in bed."

157

His eyes moved over her in slow speculation. "That doesn't sound like a half-bad idea. Are you ready to go now?" The grin that had been teasing around the corners of his mouth spread over his face in a display of wicked charm.

Without willing it, a flame of response uncurled inside Laurette, fueled by Jeff's tantalizing smile. But she made her voice firm as she said, "Absolutely not. I told you—that's over." To forestall any further arguments, she continued. "I'm going home. I'll see you in the morning."

Jeff started to speak, but was interrupted when Burris stuck his head out the back door. "You're wanted on the phone, Jeff."

Laurette used the distraction to make her exit, leaving by way of the alley while Jeff headed back into the building. She knew she had only escaped temporarily and that their discussion was far from over. And she wasn't looking forward to the next round. It was hard to remain unmoved when Jeff's voice became gentle and cajoling and his eyes whispered to her of the intimacies they had shared—and could yet share.

But she had to be strong. To fall willingly back into Jeff's arms would only amount to weakness. She wasn't the type of woman to have a casual affair, yet she knew that nothing permanent could come of this. Even if she could consider settling in Locust Grove and keeping her job at the police station, there was the far more serious problem of Jeff's work. Clearly it was very important to him. She could never put herself back in the painful situation she'd just escaped.

Laurette was so absorbed in her thoughts as she stepped out of the alley and onto Main Street that she didn't see Belinda across the street until the other woman called to her. "Got a minute?"

Blinking, Laurette brought herself back to the present. "Sure."

Belinda crossed the street, dodging between a pickup and a car. "Anything new happen at the station since I left at noon?" she asked eagerly.

Laurette shrugged. Her thoughts hadn't been on the robbery most of the day—and particularly not in the last few minutes. "Everything's so confused, I can't really tell what's happening."

The dark-haired woman looked around warily, then lowered her voice. "Listen, I've been thinking about something. What if those men who broke into the police station last night are the same ones who've been using the old shack out on West Lane? After all, Burris said they went west when they left town."

"Stockwell said they went east," Laurette countered.

Belinda chose to ignore that and continued, her eyes sparkling with excitement. "Maybe the robbers drove out to the shack and stored whatever it was they took from the stolen property room." Dropping her voice even lower, she confided, "Hannah Pearson lives just down the road from the shack and she told me she saw a light in it last night. We should go back out there and have a look."

Laurette's mouth formed a circle of surprise, but

it was a moment before she found her voice. "Oh, no! Not me! I'm not getting mixed up in anything that crazy." Maybe she'd gotten scared for no reason the last time they'd gone to the old house, but things were different today. Now men with guns might be involved.

Belinda lifted her slender shoulders in a regretful shrug. "Then I guess I'll just have to go by myself."

Laurette watched warily. Was this a con to get her to agree to go along? "You must be kidding."

"Why?"

"Because if someone *was* at the shack last night, then it's police business. Tell Jeff what you know and let him send someone out there to check."

Her eyes looking upward, Belinda seemed to be praying for patience in dealing with the village idiot. "Haven't you noticed that the town is crawling with newspaper people? This is my *one* chance to get a scoop. It could even be my ticket to a job on a big-city newspaper. If I tell Jeff about this, every reporter east of the Mississippi will end up out at that shack. Don't you understand, I've got to follow this lead on my own?"

"I understand that you want to show what kind of work you can do," Laurette said in a reasonable voice, "and I know that every job has some risks. But those men have guns! What if you're right and they *are* out there?"

Belinda was already shaking her head. "They aren't there now. They'd be crazy to hang around that shack when every cop in the state is looking for them. No, the way I've got it figured out, they

160

dumped what they stole until the heat lets up and headed out of state. That way, if they get caught, they won't have anything on them. Later they'll come back and retrieve the merchandise."

"That's just a theory," Laurette argued. "You can't be sure it's what they did, and if you're wrong, you could be walking into a dangerous situation."

Belinda was not to be daunted. "I'm ninety-nine-percent sure," she said confidently.

Laurette chewed at her lower lip and pondered the situation. As much as she didn't want to face Jeff right now, she knew the wise move would be to tell him what Belinda was up to. The other possibility was to go with Belinda and hope the shack was vacant, but Laurette didn't like the idea of gambling on that hope.

Belinda reached into her purse for her keys. "Are you coming with me or not?"

"No."

If Belinda wanted to take wild chances, that was not her responsibility, Laurette told herself. But she still felt guilty about letting Belinda go off by herself. What if something happened and she needed help? Still, what kind of help could Laurette give if she were faced with a couple of men with guns?

Without another word Belinda crossed the street and got into her hatchback, backed the car out, and headed west.

Laurette, with a rising sense of dismay, watched her go. What if the men were at the shack? What if Belinda got hurt? What if . . . The possibilities were too disturbing to consider. Turning on her heel, she dashed back to the police station.

Walley was flipping through a magazine when she burst through the door. He looked up with mild interest as she scanned the room. The rest of the men were gone.

"Where is everybody?" Laurette demanded.

"Uh, they went somewhere."

"Where?"

He stared at her with large, blinking eyes. "I'm not sure."

Distraught and confused, Laurette shoved her hand through her hair. What should she do now? With every moment that passed, Belinda was getting closer to the shack. Laurette needed a policeman, and she needed one *now.* Her distracted gaze went from Walley's rumpled uniform to the gun on his hip. Then it hit her. Walley, for all his shortcomings, *was* a policeman.

"You've got to come with me this instant," she said. "It's an emergency."

He hesitated. "There aren't any department cars outside—"

"Walley, please!"

"—and I don't like to use my own car. It's new and—"

"If you don't get up from that desk this minute, I'm going to—to set it on fire." It was the first threat that came to mind and Laurette was just upset enough to have done it. At any rate, Walley looked concerned.

"Hey, what's this about?" he asked.

"Just come! I'll explain on the way."

He rose with maddening slowness and followed her to the door. "I'm supposed to be staying here at the office taking care of things in case . . ."

Ignoring his protests, Laurette got into the front seat of his new maroon car. Walley must have finally been infected by her sense of urgency, for he trotted over to the driver's side and slid in.

"Drive out to West Lane," she directed as he started the car. "Belinda went out there and she may be walking into trouble."

As he headed out of town he surprised her by putting his foot down hard on the accelerator. Laurette found herself holding on to the dashboard while she outlined the situation. The car clattered off the rock road onto the dirt portion, kicking up a storm of dust behind them.

"Okay, slow down here." She searched along the overgrown fenceline for the turnoff. "Here! This is the road."

His mouth turned down as he gazed at the weed-jammed lane. Only a faint path showed where other cars had recently used the road. "Here?" he asked in a stricken voice. "But those branches will scratch the paint on my new car. Couldn't we park and walk?"

"It's a quarter of a mile down the lane," Laurette began, then took pity on him. "I guess if we walked straight through the fields instead of following the winding road it wouldn't be so far." Besides, it would give them the advantage of surprise.

Even before the car was stopped by the side of the road, Laurette had tumbled out and set off across a

163

field hip-high with weeds, pushing the tall grass aside with her hands as she hurried along. It didn't take long to reach the house. When she neared the old shack she saw the blue hatchback parked in front of it, but Belinda was nowhere in sight.

Laurette glanced over her shoulder toward Walley. "This is the place," she whispered. "But I don't see Belinda."

He put his hand on the butt of the gun and moved in front of her. Laurette fell back behind him, both of them crouching low as they crept up to the bedroom windows. Walley peeked into the first one and she lifted her head beside his, half dreading what she might see within. But everything looked as it had before, right down to the rusty cans on the floor.

"Let's go around back," she murmured.

He led and she followed. When she peered over the windowsill into the kitchen a cold shiver went through her. Where there had been one set of footprints before, now there were dozens laced through the dust. And where was Belinda?

"Wait here," Walley commanded. "I'll go in and see if anyone's in the basement."

She grabbed his arm and whispered fiercely. "You're not leaving me out here alone!" The open door leading to the dark basement didn't look particularly inviting, but the thought of remaining outside by herself was even less so.

He shrugged and moved to the back door. It creaked on its hinges as he pushed it open. Laurette tiptoed in behind him. If Belinda was in the house, the noise was probably scaring her to death, Laurette

164

reflected as she followed Walley to the top of the stairs, moving up closer as he pulled out a flashlight and shined it down into the blackness.

"Anyone down there?" he called.

No answer.

"Belinda? It's Laurette."

There was a rustling in the basement and then a besmudged Belinda appeared from a dark corner. Her fingers were curled around a slat of wood that she must have picked up for defense. "Thank God! Why didn't you say something the first time you beamed that light down here?"

Laurette and Walley looked at each other and then looked back down into the basement. "We just got here," Walley said bluntly.

With the flashlight shining full on her face, they both saw Belinda pale visibly. "Then who—" She swallowed hard. "Who was here before?"

Frightened, Laurette edged up so close to Walley she was practically plastered against his back. "How long ago was that?"

"A-about five minutes ago."

"There's no one but us up here. I imagine whoever you heard earlier is gone now." Walley descended the creaking steps and Laurette clattered down on his heels. As he flicked the beam of light around she saw there was nothing in the dank cobwebby basement except some old newspapers. When he started into an adjoining room Laurette and Belinda scrambled in close behind him.

"There's nothing here," he announced. "Let me

take a better look around upstairs. You two wait here."

He left, leaving them together in the dark basement. Laurette had known happier moments than the ones she spent waiting, holding her breath for the sound of a gun, a scuffle, even a stranger's voice. But all she heard was a single set of footsteps tramping about on the squeaking boards overhead.

Then Walley reappeared at the top of the steps. "Come on up. Whoever was here before definitely is gone now. We can all go back to town now."

The two women filed up the steps and out the back door. Laurette had never been so glad in her life to leave a building. "I am *never* going back in there again," she whispered to Belinda, too unsure of her voice to speak aloud.

Belinda said nothing until they reached the front of the house. "Where's your car?"

"We parked out at the road," Walley said.

"Oh, then I'll give you a ride back."

The three of them piled into Belinda's car. After they dropped Walley off at his own car Laurette stayed in the hatchback.

"I'm still shaking," she said unevenly.

"You're shaking. How do you think I feel? I was down in the basement alone when whoever that was came to the top of the stairs."

Laurette shivered at the thought of finding herself in such a situation. They drove for a few minutes in silence before she regained some of her equilibrium. "What do you think is going on?" she asked.

"I don't know, but someone is doing a lot of

tramping through that old house, so they're obviously using it for *something* and I'm positive it has a connection with what happened last night." She flashed Laurette a tentative smile. "Thanks for coming to see about me. I was losing my nerve pretty fast down in that spooky cellar. Who do you suppose was there before you and Walley arrived, and where did he go?"

Laurette shivered. "I have no idea. I'm just glad *I* didn't run into him."

They both fell back into silence for the remainder of the trip. When Belinda stopped in front of Laurette's house a phone company truck was parked in the driveway.

"Good," Laurette pronounced when she saw it. "I hope they get my billing problem straightened out."

"What's the matter?"

"The phone company's trying to charge me for scads of long distance phone calls to New York that I didn't make."

"Mmmm." Belinda's expression became speculative. "New York. I wonder if this could tie in with everything else that's going on around here?"

"I don't see how it could." Laurette got out of the car. "Try to stay out of trouble," she said with mock severity, and then added with genuine sternness, "And don't go back out to that shack again."

"Don't worry, I won't." Belinda waved to Laurette and pulled out of the driveway.

The phone repairman, a middle-aged man with sandy hair, was standing by his truck getting ready to leave when Laurette walked over to him. "Find anything wrong?" she asked.

"No. No one has tapped into your line at the pole." He scratched his head and looked perplexed. "Seems to me whoever's making the calls has got to be doing it from your house."

Laurette frowned thoughtfully. In light of all the peculiar things that had been happening around this town lately, maybe Belinda was right and the phantom caller was part of the mystery. The possibility that someone was coming into her grandfather's house brought goose bumps to her arm.

Jeff didn't get back home until midnight. By then he was so tired he kept falling asleep over the ham and cheese sandwich he'd brought from the coffee shop. Finally he put it into the refrigerator and crawled into bed.

Once there, however, it was impossible to sleep. The pillows were scented with Laurette's jasmine perfume and his body, tired as it was, began to curve to life with the thought of last night. Would Laurette have stayed the entire night if he hadn't been called away? Probably not, because of her grandfather, but he decided to ignore reality in favor of his fantasies.

Clutching a jasmine-scented pillow against him, he closed his eyes and considered what it would have been like to wake up in the morning with Laurette beside him. He knew she would look beautiful in the morning. Her eyes would be as green as the ocean and he would kiss each velvety eyelid and run his thumb over the pollen dust of her freckles. He could just imagine how her smile would dawn slowly and she would stretch like a lazy cat. They would make love fiercely. Then again, slowly. And again, passionately.

Rolling over on the bed, he chuckled aloud. Those were big plans, but he was only human. Still, he'd have liked to have had the chance to test his limits with Laurette.

His grin faded. For all he knew, last night might have been his only chance to be with Laurette. Today she had reverted to her old wariness. Okay, so her marriage hadn't worked, he thought dourly, but *he* wasn't her husband. Did she in some crazy way think that all men were alike and had decided never again to get close to any of them? Yet even while she tried to maintain a distance from him, her eyes told a different story. She seemed lonely and unsure of herself, wanting his touch, yet shying away from it.

The contradictions in Laurette's personality were complex and he was too drowsy to analyze them now. He gave up trying and fell asleep.

When Jeff walked into the station the next morning Burris was just hanging up the phone. "That was the lab," the stocky man said. "They've got some results."

Stockwell paused on the way to the coffeepot. "What'd they find out?"

"Some of the prints were ours, but there's one set they don't have on their records. They're going to check with the FBI to see if it's someone on their files."

169

"Seems like it must be," Burris mused. "This doesn't look like the work of amateurs."

"No, it doesn't," Jeff agreed, and drummed his fingers on the desk reflectively. If the robbers weren't amateurs, then they'd probably been in prison before and maybe had contacts who still were. One of the first things he'd learned as a detective was that most crimes were solved by informants. While there obviously weren't a lot of stoolies running loose in Locust Grove, Jeff still knew enough inmates in Memphis to make a trip there worth his while. Maybe one of them knew something and would talk. It was worth a try.

And while he was at it, this would be a good opportunity to professionalize Locust Grove's computer files by finding out how Memphis stored their criminal information. Laurette could make the trip with him and talk to the Memphis computer people while he visited some of his old friends behind bars. He didn't bother denying to himself that he had an ulterior motive for wanting Laurette to go to Memphis with him. They needed to spend some time alone and talk.

But how would he convince her of that? he wondered. A smile played at the corners of his mouth as the solution dawned on him.

170

CHAPTER ELEVEN

The next morning Laurette walked into the office determined to be polite but distant to Jeff. She did, however, smile at Walley on her way across to the computer. Her feelings toward him had softened considerably since he'd come to Belinda's aid yesterday. Walley merely blinked owlishly and turned back to his work. Stockwell, the only other person in the office, was more friendly.

"Hi, Laurette. You look great this morning," the tall, lean man said.

She glanced down at her maroon blazer and white wraparound skirt. "Thanks."

Jeff came into the office just as she was loading the program in the computer. "Hi," he greeted her indifferently before turning to Walley. "You'd better get back over to the stolen property room and keep doing an inventory to see if we can get some idea what those two men made off with."

She suspected Jeff was seething inwardly, because if Walley had been doing his job right, they'd already know what was missing.

Jeff left the room without so much as another

glance in Laurette's direction. Well, she thought wryly, apparently it wasn't going to be necessary to shore up her defenses against his passionate advances and entreaties. He seemed less than interested in her this morning.

Which was what she wanted, she told herself briskly. In an effort to keep from dwelling further on Jeff, she busied herself at the computer. Now that she had all the routine office data stored on discs, she was working with the far more interesting files of crime reports.

An hour later Jeff returned.

"I got through to the FBI lab," Stockwell reported. "They didn't have those mystery prints on file."

"Hmmm." Jeff scanned several forms that had been stacked on his desk. Still carrying them, he circled around to Laurette. "Listen, I'm going to go to Memphis to see if I can get any leads on who the robbers might have been. I think you should come along and talk to the data processing people at the Memphis police department."

She was completely taken aback by the suggestion. Hadn't he heard anything she'd told him yesterday? "I don't think that would be a good idea," she said firmly.

His eyes skimmed an official form. "Why not?" he asked without looking up.

"Well, I . . ." She let the words trail off and looked meaningfully toward Stockwell, who could hear every word they were saying. This was hardly the place to discuss their personal affairs.

But Jeff seemed unaware of any awkwardness.

"Why?" he repeated. "Are you busy?" Maddeningly he flipped to the next page of the sheaf of papers and continued reading.

"Not exactly." She cleared her throat self-consciously and glanced back at Stockwell. Surely Jeff realized they were being heard. With Stockwell in the room she couldn't possibly say she couldn't go because they might end up making love again and she couldn't deal with that now. Yet that accurately summed up her feelings.

Jeff finally looked up. His dark brows were lowered and he seemed genuinely confused. "Then why can't you go? It'll only be for a day or so and I might get some useful information in solving this case." He thrust his chin toward the computer. "And you could get this thing set up so it'd be compatible with the computers in Memphis. That would be a big help to the department after you're gone."

"Oh." Laurette could think of nothing else to say. He was talking about her leaving as calmly as he might discuss the weather. She hadn't expected this turn of events. Jeff, who had taken her to his bed and cradled her in his arms, suddenly seemed indifferent to her. Disoriented by his sudden change in attitude, she couldn't form her thoughts clearly.

He shuffled through the papers again. "Listen, I don't mean to push you, but I've got quite a few things to do today. I figured we'd fly to Memphis tonight and stay until Friday." He looked at his watch with a shadow of impatience, giving her the impression he was a busy man being delayed by someone who was making an issue of petty matters. "It'd be a big help to the office if you came."

Those were hardly the words of an ardent lover insisting she join him! Still, wasn't it dangerous to spend two days alone with him? Then another thought struck her—Memphis would be an ideal place to check with an employment agency and begin her search for a job. Yet she continued to hesitate, nibbling at her lower lip indecisively.

Jeff flicked another look at his watch and tapped his foot. His body language said plainly that he was a man with things to do and she was wasting his time.

Bemused, Laurette threaded her fingers through her hair and stared at the empty computer screen. While it was true that she wanted to end things between them, Jeff's sudden loss of interest stung, making her feel she couldn't have been that special to begin with if he could lose interest so quickly. Or was he simply so wound up in his work that he was oblivious to her at the moment—the way Stan used to be.

Stockwell was now looking at them with open curiosity. "Could we talk about this over a cup of coffee?" she suggested.

He looked at his watch again. "I suppose so if we make it quick."

With that gracious invitation they went across the street to the restaurant and ordered coffee. While she added cream to hers she watched him from beneath the cover of her lashes. "I'm a little curious about the way you're acting toward me today," she began tentatively.

"Oh?" He stirred in sugar. His brown eyes were a study in polite interest. Either he truly had no idea what she was talking about or he was a very good actor.

Laurette felt her way carefully. "When we talked yesterday in the alley I had the impression you wanted us to remain—well—good friends.' "

"I do."

Laurette fortified herself with a sip of coffee. "I mean *very* good friends." She couldn't quite manage to say "lovers" in such a public place, but she thought the word hung between them so forcefully, it practically screamed itself.

A look of slow comprehension dawned on Jeff's face. "Oh, I see what you're worried about." He grinned at a passing waitress before turning back to her. "Let me make this perfectly clear. I need to go to Memphis for business reasons. I hope you don't think I'm the sneaky, underhanded kind of guy who would ask you to go along as an excuse to be close to you."

Put that way, Laurette felt a little ashamed that she had thought as much.

"I want you to go because you can get some useful information in Memphis about their computer system that will help us," he continued. "Once you're gone, we won't be able to replace you with anyone nearly as proficient, so this is our last chance to get some valuable help," he concluded with an uncomplicated smile.

It was the second time today that Jeff had talked about her leaving, and Laurette wasn't sure how pleased she was by that. With a self-mocking smile she considered that for a woman who'd made up her mind to put distance between herself and Jeff, she was taking it pretty hard when he did just that. Okay, so her ego had been damaged because he could walk away from her so easily, but the end result would be what she wanted.

"Besides," Jeff continued practically, "you've been working for the town for peanuts. At least you'll get a free trip out of this." He looked at his watch again.

It certainly sounded innocent enough. At any rate, Laurette knew Jeff wasn't the kind of man to overpower her in her motel room. If anything happened between them, it would be completely mutual—except nothing was going to happen. It was strictly a business trip.

She thought again of the chance to visit an employment agency and nodded. "All right. I'll go."

"Good. I'll set it up and let you know the details later." Rising, he laid money on the table to pay for the coffee. "I hate to rush off like this, but I've got a lot of things to do."

He left her to finish her coffee alone.

That evening Laurette and Jeff climbed into a Cessna at the municipal airport and Cecil Higgins flew them to Knoxville. Jeff looked down into the misty valleys and blue-green hills of the Smokies as they flew over them. The small aircraft was so noisy that talk was practically impossible, which was fine with him.

At Knoxville he and Laurette boarded a commer-

176

cial flight to Memphis. During the flight Jeff kept the conversation friendly but impersonal. On the drive to the motel in the rented car he continued to act with a coolness he was far from feeling. With tour-guide neutrality he pointed out the sights of the city as they drove along.

"Memphis is a city of bluffs," he said in a conversational tone and pointed to a row of high bluffs by the river.

"So I see," she murmured.

He could sense her reserve, as if she might be having second thoughts about the wisdom of this trip with him. He continued his impassive narrative. "For the first hundred years Memphis was only a boom town on the border line of the West. It's just been since the early 1920s that residential areas have been laid out. Before that the residents were Chickasaw Indians who lived on the bluffs; they were here long before 1541, when De Soto visited searching for gold."

Laurette nodded with polite interest, but he didn't think she particularly cared about the city's history. He kept talking anyway. "During the Civil War Memphis was a Confederate military center. Later it was seized by Union forces."

His lecture was cut short when they arrived at the motel and checked into their separate rooms. He carried her suitcase to her door and set it outside.

"I'll meet you in a half hour to go to dinner," Laurette said. She didn't quite look at him.

"Right." Jeff sighed aloud as he watched her disappear into the motel room two doors down from his. It would have been so much cozier if she were staying in his room. All the way down on the plane he'd pretended not to notice her jasmine scent or the fact that her eyes were as green as a summer glade. Once he'd had to fight back the impulse to put his hand on her knee when she'd unconsciously turned her legs so that they were touching his.

Odd that a little over a month ago Laurette Haily had been nothing more than a girl from his past. When he'd thought of her at all it had been as a fond but distant memory. Now he scarely thought of anything except her, and she was a good deal more than a memory.

It was as if there were a space around her that was charged with an alluring electrical field. Having strayed inside that field, he had been tugged so close to her that he felt pleasure ripple through him when she laughed, and when she was unhappy his whole world turned blue. And when she talked about leaving he felt bereft and defeated. Although he'd never been in love before, that seemed to be the only word that fit the way he felt.

But he'd be damned if he was going to let her see a sign of that, or she'd bolt like a storm-shy colt. He'd have to continue to move carefully, watching her reaction at every step along the way.

Pushing open his motel door, he tossed the key onto the table and put his suitcase on the bed. After a moment's consideration he decided against changing out of his brown twill slacks and brown and white striped shirt. What he was wearing was fine for the restaurant he had in mind for dinner. Although the city was full of expensive, elegant restaurants, those were places a man took a woman when he wanted to impress her. And not wanting Laurette to think that he was trying to do that, Jeff had decided to take Laurette to a clean and bland chain restaurant.

After taking a moment to whip a comb through his hair and pat a wet washcloth over his face, he checked his watch, waited until he was a couple of minutes late, and strolled down to her door.

His knock was answered by a lilting, "Com-ing." Laurette was clipping on a gold hoop earring when she opened the door. She had traded her wrinkled traveling clothes for a yellow jersey dress that clung in all the right places. Her high heels displayed her shapely legs to excellent advantage. Her lipstick was fresh and shiny.

He was careful to hide his approval. "I thought we'd walk across the street for dinner." He jerked his head toward the chain restaurant.

She looked beyond him to the restaurant. "Oh." Her disappointment was evident.

"How does that sound?" he asked cheerfully.

"Fine," she lied without enthusiasm.

They crossed the six lanes of traffic at the nearest light, sat down at a booth near the door, and studied the plastic menu cards. "I think I'll have the veal," he decided.

"I'll have that too," she said without interest, and laid the menu aside. "Are you going to look up any old friends while you're here?" she asked.

"I'll see most of them tomorrow. I thought we'd get an early start. You can talk to the computer programmer; I'll be busy most of the day meeting with people."

"Do you have appointments with all of them?" she asked.

He smiled. "You don't need appointments to see most of the people I'll be visiting. Their days are pretty free. They're doing time in jail."

She looked puzzled. "But I thought you were trying to get information on the men who held up the station."

"I am, and that's where I stand a good chance of finding out." He was glad to have a neutral topic to discuss.

Laurette tilted her head to the side and considered this fact with the expression of a solemn child. "Will the prisoners tell you anything?"

He shrugged. "Depends who it is and what I offer in exchange. Some of them are friends, and they'll tell me because it's me who's asking. Some of them figure maybe they can make a deal with me."

"Do you make deals?" Her green eyes were wide. She seemed both horrified and fascinated by this angle of the law. "I mean, isn't that illegal?"

"No. The D.A. would have to approve any deals, but I can certainly put in a good word for anyone who's helpfully gabby."

She leaned forward and the yellow jersey eased more tightly against the swell of her breasts. He tried not to notice.

The waitress arrived then, took their orders, and disappeared. When Jeff looked back at Laurette she had her chin cupped in her hands and was regarding him with new interest. "I've never really thought much about it, but I'll bet police work can be very intriguing."

"It has its moments," he agreed mildly.

"Do you miss the excitement of being a big-city detective?"

"Sometimes," he answered honestly. "I'm happy enough right now working in Locust Grove, but I can always come back to Memphis if I want to." Or probably anywhere else. He'd had an excellent arrest record and the Memphis department had been loath to see him go.

She studied him with even greater curiosity. "How did you get shot? It doesn't bother you to talk about it, does it?" she added with an anxious look.

"Not at all. It's a pretty simple story. I was called to investigate a homicide and when I got there the killer was waiting in the bushes. It was dark and he just jumped out and pulled the trigger." He'd seen the flash of the gun but it had been several moments before he'd felt the pain in his leg.

Her eyes were soft with sympathy. "What a terrible thing to happen."

He shrugged. "I lived. There are others who aren't so lucky. And the possibility of getting shot at goes with the territory if you're a policeman."

"Then you should quit being a policeman," she said with feeling. "Why should anyone work at a job where it's open season on them every day of the year?"

"You don't understand." Jeff searched for a way to explain that helping people was what his work was all about and that for every bad person there were a lot more good people. Somebody had to protect them.

"You'd be surprised how well I understand," she said with a mirthless laugh. "It's your job and it's always going to rate first. Even after someone shot your leg out from under you you couldn't give it up."

He frowned at her. Laurette seemed to take it as a personal affront that his job meant so much to him. He watched her snapping green eyes warily. *Great, Murray,* he congratulated himself sardonically. He not only had failed to keep things impersonal, he'd made her mad. As the waitress arrived with their food, he tactfully set about trying to put things back on an even keel.

CHAPTER TWELVE

The next morning when Laurette stepped out of her motel room Jeff was standing by the pool with his back to her.

"Good morning," she called. She regretted having shown her resentment last night toward his job and was determined to be pleasant to him today.

"Hi." He turned to face her. His hands were thrust into the trouser pockets of his tan suit. With the wind tugging at his brown hair and his mouth parted in an enigmatic smile he looked like a model for *Gentleman's Quarterly*. She wished he were a little less attractive.

"Ready?" he said. "I thought we could have breakfast at the cafeteria in the basement of the police building."

"That's fine with me." It would at least be as appetizing as the nondescript restaurant where they'd eaten dinner last night.

They got into the rented car and Jeff steered it out into the thick rush-hour traffic.

"This was one of the busiest ports in the U.S. in the early 1800's." Jeff picked up the history lesson where he'd left off yesterday. "It was also the largest slave market in the central South. In 1878 a yellow fever epidemic hit and the half of the population that could afford to moved to St. Louis."

"I see," she murmured.

A short time later Jeff pulled into a new complex of city buildings and parked the car. "Here we are. I'll take you inside and introduce you to Chris Witney. He's the computer whiz. While you're with him I'll go over to the jail."

Laurette slid out of the car and followed Jeff through the wide front doors of the police department and down a long corridor. Uniformed women and men bustled past, guns on hips, whistles hanging from their necks, and faces intent. Even the people in street clothes had that same stern expression, as if years of working in the field of crime had made them grimly purposeful. Jeff nodded to several people, calling out a promise to "catch you later."

They stopped by an elevator and he pushed the Down button. After a quick breakfast in the basement cafeteria, they went upstairs to the data processing center, where they were greeted by a large man who wore Ben Franklin glasses and had a shy smile.

Jeff stood in the middle of the sleek, modern room and made the introductions. "Chris, this is Laurette Haily. Chris has been with the department since 1916," Jeff told her heartily. "He can teach you everything there is to know about police computer systems."

184

Chris turned to Laurette. "I actually came here in 1965. Jeff's always been confused about my age."

She smiled. Chris Witney's navy jacket hung in bunchy folds from shoulders that slouched forward. His tie was crooked, and a button was missing from his shirt. She liked him, disheveled appearance and all.

"Laurette," Jeff continued blithely, "knows all about computers." He motioned toward the massive disc drives and computer banks visible through a window of Chris's office, which looked over the data processing center. "She can take one of those machines apart with a screwdriver and have it fixed in no time."

"Not quite," Laurette demurred with a laugh. Jeff was in fine fettle today. He seemed boyishly happy here, which made her wonder if he secretly longed to return to a large police department. It suddenly struck her how little she knew of Jeff's hopes or future plans. They had spent time together, but they hadn't really talked about certain things that she was beginning to feel curious about.

Chris turned to Jeff. "Are you going to hang around, getting in our way?"

"Don't rush me! I'm leaving in just a minute." To Laurette he said, "I'll be back around noon."

Once Jeff was gone she and Chris settled down at a small conference table. "Okay," the large man began briskly, "since you weren't trained in police work, some of what I say may not make any sense to you. Just stop me any time you have a question."

"I will."

185

They worked straight through until ten thirty, then took a break and went back to the basement cafeteria where they both had coffee and doughnuts. They ate at a Formica table, and Chris began examining bits of thread on his shirt where a button should have been. "Jeez," he said morosely, "this was practically my last shirt that still had all the buttons."

She murmured her sympathy and tried not to let him see her smile.

"So do you like this kind of work?" Chris asked. "Being associated with the police, I mean."

Laurette blew on her steaming coffee. "I enjoy the work," she said honestly, "but I'm doing it only temporarily." She looked into his boyishly innocent face with the little Ben Franklin glasses and decided to divulge more. "In fact, as soon as we get back to your office I'd like to call an employment counselor and set up an appointment."

He didn't hide his surprise. "I'm sure Jeff will be sorry to lose you."

She busied herself wiping the sticky sugar crumbs from her fingers. "Once I get the system set up in Locust Grove he'll be able to train someone else to use it."

"But I'll *still* bet he'll be sorry to see you go," Chris pursued with a smile.

"Maybe." But if she didn't leave Locust Grove soon, her emotions were going to be so hopelessly entangled that she wouldn't be able to make a sane decision.

* * *

Jeff had called Laurette at noon to tell her he was driving out to the state prison and wouldn't be meeting her for lunch. Deciding to go to the state prison was probably a waste of time, he reflected. He hadn't learned a thing from the men doing time in the county jail and he was beginning to feel discouraged.

Once he arrived at the appropriate cellblock of the state prison, a jailer led him through a steel door at the end of a corridor, lifted a ring of keys from his belt, and fitted a key that was color-coded blue into the lock. He twisted it and swung open the heavy door.

The two men walked parallel to a long row of iron bars down a narrow hall, made a sharp left turn, and stopped in front of a cell. The jailer used the same color-coded key to open that door.

"You've got company, Rizzo."

The middle-aged man in gray prison workpants and shirt looked up from a game of solitaire. "Is it Melvin Belli?"

"No, the govenor's brought your pardon in person," the jailer retorted.

Jeff stepped into the cell. "Hi, Rizzo. How's everything?"

The jailer locked the door behind him. "Just holler when you're ready to leave. That don't include the rest of you guys," he added as he wandered off down the corridor.

Rizzo looked Jeff over head to foot. "Well, if it ain't Murray the Magnificent." Rizzo wasn't a heavy man, but he was burly, and the jowly lines on his face gave him the appearance of a morose beagle. He smiled now and the expression made him look years younger. Clapping Jeff on the shoulder, he let fly some foul language and nodded toward the cot that hung from the wall. "Sit down in the Queen Anne chair. I've sent the rest of the furniture out to be reupholstered."

Rizzo swept the cards off the cot and both men sat down.

"I've been reading about your little town in the paper," the convict said. "You're not running a very tight ship if you've got men holding up the police department."

"That's what I came to talk to you about," Jeff said. "Know anything about that?" He took out a pack of cigarettes and toyed with them.

Rizzo watched him slyly. "That depends on what it's worth to you."

Jeff tapped the cigarette pack against the palm of his hand and parried, "That would depend on what you know."

"I'm coming up before the parole board in two weeks. How good could you make my records look?"

Jeff laughed. "How bad do they look now? Never mind, don't answer that. I could put in a good word for you if you know anything worthwhile."

Rizzo bent forward, looked around conspiratorially, then said in a low voice, "Not many people know about this robbery."

That much was certainly true, Jeff agreed silently. He just hoped that Rizzo had information and that he wasn't trying to get something for nothing. "What do *you* know about it?"

"There were two of them. They had submachine guns." Rizzo looked around again as furtively if he had confided a top Pentagon secret to a Russian spy.

"That was in the paper," Jeff pointed out.

"I know, but here's something you don't know. The stuff they're stealing is coming out of New York."

Jeff was instantly alert. "What is this 'stuff?' "

"I'm not sure. My informants don't know yet," Rizzo added. His chest had swelled with importance. "But there's one other thing. There's an inside man on this job."

Jeff's jaw went slack as he stared at the convict. "You mean someone in the police department?"

"That's right." Rizzo smiled smugly. "Just 'cause a man's a cop don't mean you can trust him." He seemed to take such great delight in making that statement that he repeated it. "No, sir, just 'cause a man's a cop don't mean you can trust him."

"Do you know who the inside man is?" Jeff demanded.

Rizzo shook his head. "Naw. Just that there is one."

Jeff mulled this over silently. It was possible, of course. But he found himself resisting the idea that one of the men who worked under him could be a criminal. "You're *sure?*"

Rizzo was affronted. "When someone knocked over the Fifth National Bank in Knoxville, who fingered the birds? Rizzo. When they gunned down old Pappy Giovanni in the streets of Nashville, who told the cops where to look? Rizzo. If it weren't for me, you guys wouldn't solve any crimes." He leaned back and folded his arms across his chest, his expression sullen.

Jeff laughed. "You're being too modest, Rizzo."

"Yeah, well, you can laugh, but I'm the one in the know."

Jeff didn't deny that Rizzo had connections and he usually knew what was going on in the streets even when he was behind stone walls and iron bars—which don't necessarily a prison make, but they go a long way toward it.

"Okay, thanks, Rizzo. You've been a big help. I'll talk to the warden on my way out."

Rizzo stood when Jeff did. "When you see him, tell him the food's crummy."

Jeff called for the guard, who appeared moments later and unlocked the cell.

"Tell him to hire Julia Child to do the cooking."

Jeff chuckled. "I'll pass the word along."

Rizzo was still shouting after them as Jeff walked down the stark prison corridor and out through the clanking metal door. He walked mechanically beside the guard, paying scant attention to Rizzo's comical requests or the sights and smells of the prison. In his mind he was busy reviewing the men who worked for the Locust Grove police department. Depressing as the thought was, one of them might be guilty of conspiracy with the two armed robbers.

Laurette silently added butter to her baked potato and took a small bite. She and Jeff were seated at an intimate table in a dimly lit restaurant with accents from Medieval England. The service was excellent, the food superb, and the old-world atmosphere charming. She had suggested the restaurant on Chris's recommendation. After seeing Jeff's choice of restaurants last night, she certainly wasn't going to leave such decisions to him.

Jeff had seemed surprised by her selection, but had been agreeable. And he had dressed properly. In fact, he looked very suave in a wine-red jacket and crisp white shirt. His brown hair was parted on one side and lay in even, unruffled layers. The flickering candle on their table danced across his face, accenting his dark eyes before retreating again to leave them in shadow. He was the picture of a handsome escort.

In fact, when Laurette had first opened her motel door and seen him looking so utterly captivating, she'd had to remind herself this was a business trip. Yet from the moment they'd gotten into the rental car, Jeff had been remote and brooding, giving only absent replies to her light remarks.

At first she'd been puzzled, but now something closer to anger was surfacing. Crumpling her napkin, she leaned forward abruptly. "Look, if you don't want to be here with me, then say so and we can leave right now."

He stared at her. "What are you talking about?"

"I'm talking about the way you're acting. I know we agreed to keep our relationship strictly professional, but even business acquaintances treat each other with civility. You've been indifferent to me since we started this trip, and you're being downright rude this evening."

The candlelight wavered back toward him and she saw his chocolate brown eyes widen. "I'm sorry. I didn't mean to be."

Laurette was only slightly mollified. "Well, you were," she mumbled.

He ran his fingers through his hair, disturbing the perfect layers and absently restyling it into a more casual look. "It's just that I have some other things on my mind. I've found out something about the robbery," he elaborated.

She immediately forgot her chagrin at being ignored. "You did? Can you tell me?"

His eyes met hers directly then. "If what my informant says is true, someone on our local police force helped plan the robbery."

She fell back against her chair as if she'd been shoved backward. "Who?"

He shook his head. "I don't know." In a rougher voice he added, "But I'm going to find out. From now on every person there is under suspicion."

It took a moment for that statement to fully sink in. Startled and defensive, Laurette fumbled for words, "I—I hope you don't think that I—that *I* had anything to do with this."

Without warning, a smile blazed across his face and he laughed. "No, I don't. You're one of the few people in the world I trust absolutely, Etty. You're the only one I'd tell this to."

"Oh." It touched her that his faith in her was so deep. "You make me feel humble," she murmured. "I'm not sure I'm worthy of such implicit trust."

His smile softened. "You are."

His gaze continued to hold hers and she could do nothing but look back into his rich brown eyes and feel herself being pulled into a swirl of feelings. She was intensely aware of the thick fringe of his lashes, the sculpted cheekbones accented by the candlelight, and the generous curve of his mouth. Everything about him was perfect, and the woman in her responded not only to his masculine beauty but to the beauty of his soul.

The resolve not to become involved with him weighed on her like a heavy winter coat. But when she looked at him smiling she no longer felt the need for such protection. She smiled back at him.

"Are you finished eating?" he asked quietly.

"Yes."

He nodded toward the private bar that adjoined the restaurant. In a corner of the room a three-piece band played a soft waltz and several couples danced on a tiny parquet floor. "Would you like to dance?"

"I'd like that very much," she said softly.

He rose and pulled back her chair. She floated onto the dance floor and lifted her hand to rest on his shoulder while he drew her close into the circle of his arms and they began to glide in time to the music.

They didn't always move in correct time with each other, but it didn't matter. If one of them made a mistake, they merely smiled at each other, moved closer together, and continued performing their own version of the waltz. Tonight she was living a dream and nothing could be wrong.

"I'm glad you were here tonight." Jeff's words were a whisper against her ear that sent little flames

193

of heat running down her spine. "I didn't want to be alone."

"I know." She realized it had shaken him to find out one of his own men was a criminal, but she also knew his reasons for wanting to be with her were far more complex than that—just as her own reasons for wanting to be with him were layered with need as well as a desire to give.

They danced on in silence, having at last found the rhythm within themselves so that they no longer moved in different directions. Now their bodies spun and turned in time. He reached out to stroke back a single strand of her hair that had strayed from the rest, and she curved her hand around the nape of his neck. His hand slid lower on her hip and rested there with easy intimacy. They traded quiet, private smiles.

Other couples drifted on and off the dance floor, but Laurette and Jeff stayed. This was the boy she'd had a crush on as an adolescent when she had been awakening to the wonders of the opposite sex. Her feelings now were as breathless and tumultuous as they'd been then, and she felt a sense of completeness at having come full circle to discover that the boy who had engendered such worshipful admiration had become a man who inspired the same feelings.

She rested her head on his chest. Whatever happened tonight would happen. She wasn't going to try to control herself or fate. If she looked back with regret tomorrow, then that would be tomorrow, and she would deal with it then. But at this moment she was exactly where she wanted to be.

Jeff's hands moved over her hip and the satiny fabric of her skirt whispered like a distant wind. She looked up at him and saw that his eyes were filled with tenderness. The band played another song, faster and with a swing. She and Jeff continued to waltz.

CHAPTER THIRTEEN

Jeff parked in front of the door of his motel room and turned to Laurette. She went willingly into his arms and they kissed gently, as though they had all the time in the world for passion and could therefore afford the luxury of unhurried kisses.

Each touch, each pause to look into each other's eyes, had a special quality that made it as rewarding as the actual act of consummation. Their kisses weren't deliberately building to anything specific, although each knew what was ultimately to come. At the same time they were savoring each kiss and caress for its own value.

His lips covered hers with rich, deep kisses, then moved off into the hollow of her cheek before coming to rest and nibble at her ear. While his fingers trailed through her hair she strummed her hand along the square line of his jaw and followed with powdery kisses.

"Let's go inside," he said in a passion-seared voice.

"Let's," she agreed huskily.

He opened her car door and led her to his room. When she closed the door the room was plunged into pitch blackness. They sank onto the bed together and her head fell back against the pillow. He followed her down, covering her mouth with his and soaking her thirsty lips with kisses. She shifted on the bed, allowing his form to fit closer against hers as her lips parted and his tongue slid between them.

For what could have been hours or might have been moments the only sound was their breathing. Laurette could feel his body coming to life against hers. It was the most intoxicating sensation she'd ever felt in her life. And while his body became firmer she felt her own relaxing into soft readiness. She wanted him, but the anticipation was almost as exciting as being enfolded within his body. Almost.

His hands roved over her, exploring the silky skin of her legs and pushing back her dress to tease up against the smooth flesh of her thighs. But he didn't take her dress off or remove his own clothes. Laurette's hands slid over his sinewy curves and hard-coiled muscles while her mouth remained fastened to his, drinking in his kisses.

Her hand finally came to rest low on his stomach and his breathing became more urgent. As she let her fingers move with womanly purpose, he dragged her closer against him, then abruptly released her, stood, and shed his clothes. Laurette started to rise and remove hers also, but he returned and pinned her back on the bed.

While her dress rustled against the sheets he drew her into his arms and covered her face with kisses. He pushed the skirt of her dress aside and his hands began stroking her thighs. She caught her breath and waited with a sense of awe as his hands moved upward with clear intent. She felt her body become hot and pliant and eager as his hands continued their magic.

Even as she was swept up in the moment a part of her marveled that with only a few well-placed touches he had made her body unfold like a blossoming flower. Even her breasts had grown taut and aching, crying out for a release that only his body could give. But still he waited, postponing the moment of union until she was so ripe and swollen with need that she felt almost bereft. And then he filled her and she felt a glorious sense of relief.

It was replaced almost instantly by a new hunger. He was part of her now and arousing currents of desire, but she knew this was just a prelude to the greater joy that would be hers. He lifted her closer to him, handling the weight of her body as if it were of no significance. For some reason that excited her. His muscular, hairy legs brushed against her smooth ones. That excited her too. She smothered his shoulder in biting little kisses as his hands played over her, stopping to fondle and caress before moving on.

The sensations rising to the surface from deep inside her were only partly physical. No other man but Jeff could have reached into her and found the means to awaken such exquisite emotions. He knew exactly when to move and just when to pause to drive her even further toward the brink of euphoria. He lifted her closer to him and she felt her control slipping. The tempo of their body rhythms became faster and her control slipped further.

She clutched him as tightly as she could and felt the cool smoothness of his back. She wanted to tell him not to stop—to never stop—but the words were lost in her throat and escaped only as inarticulate moans of pleasure. And then he reached deep within her and suddenly she was spinning off the planet and out into ecstasy.

His mouth recaptured hers and she returned his kisses frantically, trying to hold every part of him to her so that he, too, could feel the explosions of pleasure that shook her. In her mind's eye she could see fireworks shattering colors of red and gold and blue against the darkness. The fragments of colors seemed so vivid and real, she was sure he must be able to see them. And she was certain he was experiencing the same throbbing physical delight, for she could feel his body taut and shuddering against hers, his back damp with moisture.

She continued to cling to him as the colors faded and the delicious swirl within subsided to a pleasurable afterglow.

After they had reluctantly parted, she lay with her arms clasped around his neck and her head resting on his shoulder. The silence between them was thick with the pleasure of unspoken words of happiness.

"You're not going to leave this time, are you?" he finally asked in a rich, teasing voice.

"You're not going to get a phone call, are you?" she parried with a laugh.

"No. And if I did, I wouldn't go."

Laurette didn't know if that was true or not, but it pleased her that he had said it. She pressed a kiss on his chest, then turned to rest her cheek there. "Did you have this in mind when you asked me to come to Memphis?"

"I had hopes."

Laurette mulled that over a moment, then raised up to pummel him with her hands. "You sneak! You told me that this was only a business trip."

Laughing, he captured her hands. "I lied," he said without a trace of repentance.

Her words were stifled when his mouth covered hers in a hard, insistent kiss. After token resistance she joined in, and the kiss softened into an infinitely more exciting struggle. She threaded the tip of her tongue between his lips and had the gratification of hearing him moan and pull her closer. Her hands moved to encircle his waist and she pulled him back to cover her body.

"What if this hadn't happened?" She played with the tiny hairs at the nape of his neck. "Did you have an alternate plan?"

"Nothing definite, but I was prepared to be ingenious. I love it when you stroke my back," he added, and helpfully moved her free hand low on his back. "Where was I?" he wondered.

"You were telling me the devious ways you thought up to lure me into your bed." With her index finger she played little circles on the small of his back.

"I'm only human," he complained. "You could hardly expect me to watch you sitting at that computer every day all perfumed and pretty, wearing those classy dresses and *not* start getting devious." He scattered random kisses over her face.

She sighed. As disturbing as the truth was, she felt compelled to tell him. "Tonight is tonight and it's wonderful, but I can't give any guarantees about tomorrow."

"Right now I don't want any," he said hoarsely. "I just want this moment."

"So do I." She kissed his navel and tasted salty dew, then rolled her hands around the curve of his shoulder and felt the firm texture of his skin made silky by the sheen of moisture. That excited her. Everything about Jeff excited her. Her body craved his with an almost primitive need.

She lifted her head and brought her mouth back to his. Their lips touched briefly, flitted away, and then returned hungrily. This time when his hands moved over her bare skin he was rougher and more demanding. She understood. She felt the same barely restrained desire, as if their first lovemaking had been but a prelude to this more fiery, almost violent union. When they came together again they moved against each other in a wild rhythm that took Laurette to a new plateau and left her even more breathless than the first time.

Together they finally sank back against the tortured sheets. "You're going to kill me, Etty, but what a way to go!"

She giggled and moved into the security of his arms. "I don't think I'll do any permanent damage. You seem pretty healthy."

"We should have made arrangements to stay in

Memphis longer. I had no idea it was going to be like this."

"But you had hopes," she reminded him tartly. Not that she begrudged him those. The evening was turning out exquisitely.

"Yes, lots of hopes." His hands strayed over her full breasts, proceeded to her flat stomach, and continued on down to her thighs. "You're quite a woman, Etty. I can remember when you were as flat as a stick."

"And I can remember when you sent away for a Charles Atlas course," she said. Her palms glazed down the wall of his chest and onto his taut stomach. "I believe it paid off too," she murmured appreciatively.

"At least I'll have a little time tomorrow to show you the town. Are you and Chris finished going over the computer stuff?"

"Yes." She bit her lip. Tomorrow morning she had an appointment with an employment counselor, but she didn't want to mention that to Jeff. Not now. That was the future and she wouldn't let it interfere with tonight. She only said, "I have something else scheduled in the morning, but I'll be free at noon. I'd love to see the city."

"Good." He nuzzled against her neck. "We can start with a thorough examination of my motel room."

Her voice rippled with suppressed laughter. "Over my dead body."

"I'd prefer that you took a more active role, Etty." His voice was husky with sensuality.

202

He pulled a feather out of the pillow and used it to tickle her nose. She had to use the whole pillow to pound him back into submission.

"Now, where was I?" she asked with duchesslike formality. "Oh, yes, I was going to tell you my suggestion about how to find out which one of the policemen is part of the robbery conspiracy. If you start asking questions, they'll know you suspect one of them, but if I ask a few innocent questions, no one will think—"

"No!" His word echoed against the walls and probably woke up the neighbors on either side of them.

She hesitated, then tried again cautiously. "But I'd just—"

"Absolutely not!" he exploded. "I won't have you putting yourself in danger."

She raised up on her elbow. Now that her eyes were accustomed to the dark, she could just make out his dim outline. "I won't be putting myself in danger. I'll pretend to be mildly curious, that's all. You'd be surprised what men will tell a woman who shows some interest in what they're doing. And whoever it is is probably dying to brag."

"Etty, I forbid you to get involved in this," he said sharply.

She pulled her mouth into a stubborn line, but said nothing.

"Okay?" he demanded.

Mutinously she shook her head. "No, it's not okay. I'm not a nitwit who'll make it obvious what

I'm trying to find out. I plan to use tact and diplomacy to get the information."

"I don't care if you plan to use thumbscrews and blackjacks, I don't want you asking *anyone* anything. Whoever did this is fine-tuned to even the most innocent questions. And he means business or he wouldn't be running around with men who carry submachine guns. You stay out of this and leave it to me."

Laurette mumbled something that he seemed to accept as agreement. But she still felt she was the person in the best position to help. And a few very innocent questions couldn't hurt.

As they lay in silence wrapped in their own thoughts, Laurette mentally reviewed the policemen on the Locust Grove force, trying to determine who the culprit might be. When she got to Walley she paused to consider him more closely.

"Do you think it's Walley?" she asked.

Jeff answered with another question. "Why do you suggest him?"

"Because he doesn't mingle with the other men and he seems to have a chip on his shoulder."

"I've thought about him," Jeff admitted.

"And he has a brand-new car," Laurette added, and then felt guilty as she recalled that Walley had used that car to take her out to West Lane to make sure Belinda was all right. Just because Walley wasn't the world's most social creature didn't mean he was a crook. "It may not be him," she pointed out.

Jeff didn't reply.

She felt compelled to defend Wally further. "I

don't know if he told you, but he took me out to West Lane the other day. I was worried because Belinda had gone out there alone. She thought the gunmen might be using it as a drop for stolen goods."

"He told me," Jeff said.

It was difficult to read his tone. "Well," she continued, "Walley went right in there with his gun drawn. I hadn't expected that, and I have to admit I was impressed."

He was silent.

"I think maybe you've shortchanged him," she pursued. "He handled the whole thing professionally."

"If he were professional at all, he wouldn't have let you go along," he snapped. "I want you to stay out of this mess, Laurette. Do you understand?"

His steely tone suggested that argument would be futile. She could just picture the grim set of his jaw.

"Yes, I understand." She tucked her body against his. She wasn't going to waste time arguing when their time could be better spent.

Jeff was already awake when Laurette started to slide noiselessly out of bed. He wrapped an arm around her and pulled her back until she was fitted against him.

"G'morning." He nuzzled his chin against her honey blond hair.

"Good morning." He could hear the smile in her voice. "Now let me go."

He immediately tightened his hold on her. "Never!"

* * *

"Jeff, I've got to get up," she protested. "There's something I want to do this morning."

"There's something I want to do this morning too," he informed her with a wicked chuckle.

"Jeff . . ." It was half command, half plea.

He relented. "Where are you going?" he asked as she slipped from the bed and he rolled onto his back, putting his hands behind his head to watch her. Her body was bare and he studied it with the appreciation of a connoisseur while she searched for her clothes on the floor.

She didn't answer his question directly. "Back to my room to get dressed."

"Why so early?"

Laurette sighed, dragged a cover off the bed, and wrapped it around herself before turning back to him. "I have an appointment with an employment counselor at nine."

She was waiting for him to object, Jeff realized. He wanted to, but something told him that would be a mistake. He knew that seeing an employment counselor meant Laurette was making specific plans for a future that didn't include him, but he wasn't going to dwell on that now. Last night they had shared something rare and beautiful and he was not going to do anything to shatter the fragile relationship they were establishing.

"How are you going to get there?" he asked with nothing more than friendly interest. She seemed to relax, apparently relieved that he was not going to argue.

"I'll take a cab."

Shaking his head, Jeff threw back the sheet and began dressing. "No sense in that. I'll drive you."

Laurette bit her lower lip and looked at him uncertainly. "You don't have to do that."

He zipped his pants and began putting on his socks. "I don't mind," he said easily. "I'll drop you there, then go over to the station to catch up on some visiting. You can call me there when you're through."

She smiled weakly. "Thanks."

Laurette was still standing with the sheet draped around her and he realized she felt self-conscious about dressing in front of him. He wanted to take her into his arms and kiss her until she let the sheet drop and led him back to the bed, but he knew that wasn't going to happen. Last night's mood of intimacy had been broken and she was once again reserved and uncertain. He stifled a sigh.

Rising, he started into the bathroom. "Go ahead and put some clothes on. I'll brush my teeth."

He heard her breathe her relief as he closed the bathroom door.

The employment agent was a substantial-looking Teutonic woman named Helga. She beamed with enthusiasm as she skimmed Laurette's résumé.

"Oh, my dear, you have all the right qualifications. You not only have a business degree, but you know computers!"

Laurette leaned forward in the plush suede chair.

"I'm not particularly anxious to work in that field again."

Helga's look was accusing, as if Laurette had personally thwarted her. "But you said that's what you're doing at the police station in"—she waved a hand vaguely—"in wherever that town was."

"Locust Grove, but that's only a temporary job," Laurette explained.

"Do you like it?"

"Well, yes," Laurette admitted truthfully, "but I'm not going to make a *career* of it."

Helga nodded with the absent attention of a mother who knew what was best for a difficult child. "Of course you don't want to make a career out of work in some backwoods town, but you *do* want to use your computer skills. And with your experience and education the possibilities are endless. Now then, I'm going to begin making some phone calls right away. I expect to have good news for you shortly." Helga beamed at her.

Laurette thanked her and left.

Standing outside the building waiting for Jeff, Laurette shifted her purse strap to a more comfortable position on her shoulder as her thoughts returned to last night. She hadn't intended for it to happen but, Lord help her, now that it had she could hardly wait to be with Jeff again. It was all so confusing! How could she look at job opportunities that might take her far away from him? Yet how could she *not* leave Locust Grove when staying meant that she would only become more and more emotionally entangled with a man who was in love with his job

. . . and a man who had never said he was in love with her.

Laurette saw the maroon car pull into the parking lot and walked toward it.

"Hi." Jeff greeted her with a wide smile. "How did it go?"

"Fine," she said evasively. To keep him from asking further questions, she said brightly, "We have the whole afternoon to ourselves. I want you to give me the grand tour of the town."

"Let's start by getting something for lunch."

If Jeff was curious about what she'd found out from the employment agent, he didn't show it. Instead, they made casual conversation while he drove to a restaurant on Beale Street.

When they were seated at an oak table near a fern-shrouded window, Jeff pointed outside. "I once spent three days on stake-out right across the street. I was a blind musician." A smile stole over his face and his eyes darkened in amusement. "The police department gave me the only instrument they could find lying around. It was a harmonica and of course I couldn't play worth a damn. Shopkeepers came out and tried to run me off and one man passing on the street gave me a buck if I promised to quit playing."

She grinned and felt herself relax. If Jeff was unhappy about her appointment, he wasn't showing it. Maybe he had already resigned himself to the fact she was leaving.

"What other disguises did you assume?" she asked.

"I was a woman once."

Laurette cocked one eyebrow. "Really?"

"A blonde," he recalled with a devilish smile. "A hooker."

"My, this is interesting." She toyed with her gold bracelet and added, "You must have been something of a disappointment to the men when they got you into a hotel room."

His smile deepened. "They were even more disappointed when I got them into a jail cell."

A smile played around her lips as Laurette studied Jeff. With his square-cut features, wide shoulders, and deep voice he was completely masculine. She couldn't imagine him playing the part of a woman. She especially couldn't imagine that when she thought about last night. He'd been very masculine then. Thinking about it sent a little shiver down her spine. Already she was looking forward to tonight.

The question of where this affair would end was not something she wanted to consider now. She was content to sit across the table from Jeff, watch him push back the hair that slid across his forehead, and listen to him talk.

They finished their meal and lingered over coffee, talking with the ease of old friends. But Laurette knew there was an added quality to their closeness that had nothing to do with the fact that they'd known each other as children; it was based on what they knew of each other as man and woman.

"Ready to see the rest of the town?" Jeff finally asked.

She nodded.

They left the restaurant and strolled around Beale

Street, stopping at PeeWee's Saloon, where W. C. Handy had created the blues. The area was now a shopping district and they took time to go into the stores to browse around.

Next they went to Victorian Village and toured several of the quaint old houses. Laurette exclaimed over the gingerbread decoration, the round towers, and the stained glass in the windows. She thoroughly enjoyed every minute of the tour, but then, she thought she would have enjoyed touring a swamp as long as she was with Jeff.

And always there was the unspoken promise of tonight.

CHAPTER FOURTEEN

They arrived back at the motel at nine o'clock. "Want to come down to my room for a drink?" Jeff suggested.

Her eyes twinkled. "I didn't know you had anything to drink."

"I have water," he offered hopefully. "And I'll call room service for ice."

Smiling, she moved to his side and felt the pleasant weight of his arm over her shoulder. Together they walked into his dark motel room.

Without turning the light on he pulled her into his arms and kissed her forehead, grazed her cheeks, and continued on down to sample her lips. Laurette wrapped her arms around his waist and gave herself over to the tantalizing kiss.

She felt his hunger quicken as his mouth moved over hers, pressing more urgently against her lips before sliding the tip of his tongue between them. His hands moved up and down her back, stopping now and then to curve around her side and draw her closer to him until their hips touched and she felt his taut stomach against her own. Their kiss lengthened and evolved in a dewy exchange of passion.

Laurette was floating in such a haze of pleasure that he was slipping her dress from her before she was aware he had unfastened it. It crumpled to the floor in a flutter of fabric and was followed by the soft swish of her slip and silken undergarments. In a matter of seconds she was completely unclothed. She helped him with the buttons of his shirt, then curled up in the bed and waited for him while he sat on the edge and took off his socks and trousers. When he turned to her, she went readily into his arms, already breathless for his kisses.

"This is the only time I really understand you," he said as he moved slowly into her.

She caught her breath at the unexpectedness of their union. He brushed back her hair, bent to kiss her breasts, then stirred inside her. Again she caught her breath. They had been together before, but she'd never been so intensely aware of what it meant for their bodies to merge as one. She felt a sense of awe at knowing his feelings for her were so strong that she could control his body—and he hers. His lips flickered across hers and he moved within her again. A sheet of bliss rolled over her and she wanted to talk to him, to tell him how she felt, but already she was slipping deeper into that soft and violent heat and her breathing was checkered and irregular.

With his every moment she felt another swell of euphoria rippling over her until their bodies were melding in chaotic time and the sheets were coming so close together they were smothering her. She lifted her body even closer to his and felt an explosion of passion and heard the husky cry of her name. Her own lips moved soundlessly, trying to say his, trying to say how wonderful she felt, but it was left to her body to say that for her.

After the flash and fire of lovemaking she nestled against the warm wall of his chest and let her fingertips roam up and down his arm.

"Memphis was never so enjoyable before," he whispered against the top of her head.

With a soft smile she trailed her hands over his rib cage. "Were you dating anyone then?" she asked, surprised at herself for wanting to destroy this moment with such a question.

"Oh, sure, I dated other women," he said casually and paused to kiss the tip of her nose. "But it was never like this before. I think I knew from the minute I saw you again that it would be special between us."

Laurette's hands stilled on the smooth flesh of his abdomen. Jeff's words were pulling her out of the spell of the moment and forcing her to think of the future.

He slid his hands up and down her bare back in an absent caress as he continued reflectively. "Being a policeman can be a lonely job. You learn not to trust too many people. Someone's always trying to get you to fix a ticket or use your influence for them in other ways." His hand stroked low and cupped around her bottom. "But I never had an instant of doubt about you. I knew when we met that my life was going to change for the better." He kissed her forehead. "And it has."

Overcome by a spasm of guilt, Laurette bit her lip. He trusted her, yet she had not told him about Grandfather's still. "Oh, Jeff, I don't know what to say. I'm touched, but I just don't know about the future and—"

"Shh." He pressed his index finger against her lips. "You don't have to say anything. I just wanted to tell you how I feel."

Nodding wordlessly, she snuggled closer into the shelter of his arms. She was so moved by his words that tears misted in her eyes. She also felt humbled by his honesty and upset by her own lack of sensitivity. She'd been so busy worrying about herself and how a relationship might affect her that she hadn't stopped to consider Jeff's feelings. Yet he was surely as vulnerable as she.

In many ways they were alike. He had been injured in Memphis and had gone back to Locust Grove to put his life back together. Although her scars were less visible, she'd gone to Locust Grove for the same reason. He'd found a satisfying job there, but he hadn't found companionship or love, and he must have been as lonely as she.

Jeff's arm went slack around her and his breathing fell into the regular cadence of sleep. She remained nestled against him, wanting to give him some kind of comfort to make up for the loneliness he'd suffered. But even now, even when she was so touched at seeing things from his point of view, she knew she couldn't make any promises.

But for the first time, she was willing to look at remaining in Locust Grove as an option. Perhaps she and Jeff could work things out, she thought, and felt the tremendous relief of someone who has been given a reprieve from a life sentence. Tomorrow on the plane they would talk, she promised herself, and went to sleep, smiling blissfully.

Morning came quickly. Amid a flurry of luggage and boarding passes, she and Jeff started back to Locust Grove. Once on the plane Jeff flipped open the locks on his briefcase, drew out several papers, and began making notes in the margin.

She watched him in silent dismay. "What are you doing?" she finally asked.

"Making notes on some things to check on when I get back. I have a couple of strong hunches to follow."

Something thudded in the pit of her stomach like a rock hitting the bottom of a deep canyon. Jeff was eager to get home and delve back into the robbery. She'd seen that same look of excited concentration on Stan's face. Suddenly last night, with all of its hope and confidences, seemed far away.

She had to be realistic about this, she told herself. As a policeman his work was important to him. She must accept that. He'd told her she was special to him, but his work was also special. Still, she couldn't help wondering that if it came to a choice, which would he choose?

Jeff made a notation on the paper, then turned to her. "Tell me, would it be possible for you to plot locations on the computer?"

Surprised by the question, she answered slowly,

"The computer has graphic capabilities so, yes, it could be used for plotting."

"Hmmm." He squinted in thought. "Then we could plot the locations where moonshine has been found and learn where the concentration of it is strongest. That might give us a clue to where it's coming from."

The still! Laurette felt disoriented as she groped for words. "But—but I thought you were trying to find the robbers."

"I'm working on that too," he said matter-of-factly. "But it occurred to me this is a terrific way to use the computer." He glanced about and she could tell he didn't want to say too much. "Besides, just because making moonshine may not be in the same league with armed robbery, I don't intend to close my eyes to it. Whoever is running that still has been getting away with it long enough and it's time to put a stop to it."

Laurette flicked her tongue over her dry lips. Jeff was sitting up straight and his profile was a study in chiseled lines. Nothing about his face invited confidence or suggested leniency. Yet, she reminded herself, this was a man she'd shared a bed with. She had seen his gentle, caring side. Surely she could tell him about her grandfather.

Then she remembered what he had told Burris about not giving preferential treatment to anyone. Wearily she rested back against the cushions. If only she understood Jeff better. But sometimes she felt she didn't know him at all. He had surprised her by diving back into his work as soon as they'd boarded the plane today. After last night she had expected him to be warmer, or closer, or more attentive . . .

She shifted on the narrow airplane seat. Kathy had once suggested that Jeff immersed himself in his work because that was all he had. Maybe it was true. Perhaps he was even afraid of becoming too close to her. After all, she had made it clear from the beginning that she didn't plan to stay long in Locust Grove. Knowing that, what sensible man wouldn't guard himself against being hurt?

But what about his words last night? a frustrated voice inside her demanded. What had their nights together meant to him? The questions had no ready answer; they only brought up other questions. Laurette felt lost in a maze where every path she chose led either to a dead end or took her deeper into the labyrinth.

"I want you to start working on the plotting as soon as you get back to work," Jeff said.

Her wandering thoughts landed squarely back to her grandfather and the problem of his still. She had tried before to find it, but she would have to try harder or Jeff might very well find it first. "I'll get right on that." If he noticed the hollowness in her voice, he said nothing. Laurette turned away from him and pretended to go to sleep.

Finally the drone of the airplane did lull her to sleep and she didn't awaken until the plane touched down in Knoxville. There they changed into a small plane and flew to the municipal airport in Locust

Grove, where they were met by a squad car driven by Burris.

Jeff chatted with him while he drove Laurette home. When they reached her grandfather's house Jeff turned to her with a smile. "It was a productive trip. I hope you can use the information Chris gave you." With an enigmatic smile he added, "I know I can certainly use what I learned."

"Yes," she murmured. As she watched the car pull away she wondered about his last statement. Had he meant he could use what he'd learned about her to get closer to her? Or was she only reading something into his words?

Sighing, she marched up the porch stairs carrying her suitcase. Her feelings toward Jeff seemed to be in hopeless turmoil. As the screen door banged shut behind her she heard the sounds of someone in the kitchen.

"Grandfather, I'm home," she called.

There was no answer.

"I'm home," she repeated, set her suitcase down, and started toward the kitchen.

She heard the back door being thrown open, followed by the sound of running footsteps. "What the . . ." she exclaimed, and rushed into the kitchen. The back door stood wide open.

Had it been her grandfather who had bolted? But that hardly seemed likely. A quick survey of the counters showed there were no mason jars in sight. Besides, even if he'd had the complete still set up in the kitchen, he wouldn't have run away from her.

More to the point, she didn't think her grandfather could move that fast.

Puzzled, she approached the back door. If the person in the kitchen hadn't been her grandfather, then whom had she surprised? Someone who had come to the house to buy moonshine? A burglar? She trembled at that possibility.

Immediately her eyes flew to the open door. Was someone even now lurking in the backyard? The question sent a chill through her. There were plenty of overgrown patches in the garden where a crouching man could hide, or he could easily be behind one of the outbuildings. She fought back at her fears and forced herself to be logical. Probably whoever had been in the house had jumped the fence onto the sidewalk and was now a block away, walking with a casual jaunt. But who had the intruder been and what had he wanted? It was an eerie feeling to know a stranger had been in the house only moments before.

Laurette started to shut the door, then paused, remembering that Jeff had dusted the station looking for fingerprints of the robbers. There might be fingerprints on this doorknob. Leaving the door ajar, she circled the kitchen. There seemed to be nothing amiss in the kitchen. The same was true in the seldom-used dining room. Likewise the living room. She was almost out of the living room on her way to the stairs when a thought struck her. Pivoting, she walked to the phone.

The receiver rested serenely on its cradle, but she stared at it hard, as if willing it to yield a clue. Was it possible that whoever had bolted from the kitchen was the same person who had been making all the long distance calls from this telephone?

Whatever the answer to that question, this was a job for the police. She started to pick up the phone to dial, then hesitated. Jeff suspected someone on the police force was crooked, so she couldn't call them. The only person she could confide in was Jeff, but she couldn't use the phone to do it because she would destroy any prints that happened to be on the phone. She would have to go see him personally.

Laurette was pulled out of her thoughts by the sound of the front door opening. She looked up to see Grandfather entering. His white hair was partially hidden by his best fedora and he was wearing a good, if baggy, pair of pants.

"Hello, child." He didn't smile, but she could see the affection in his eyes and she knew he was glad she was back.

"Hi, Grandfather." She kissed him on the cheek, then put her arms around him and hugged him tightly. Beneath his oversize clothes he felt thin and frail. That brought out her protective streak and made her determined to find out who'd been in this house today. Anyone bold enough to walk into a house in broad daylight might be deadly if surprised. And Grandfather wasn't strong enough to defend himself.

"Did you have a good trip?" he asked as she released him and stepped back.

"It was fine." Her bland words revealed nothing about the moments of bliss with Jeff or her later confusion. With studied indifference she asked, "Did you go out the back door a minute ago?" She didn't think it had been Grandfather, but she had to make sure.

"No. I jest this minute got back from Mountain View."

The fear she had been trying to fight back resurfaced. She was definitely going to tell Jeff. "I've got to run out and see someone. I'll be gone for a few minutes. By the way," she added casually, "there was a funny smell in the kitchen, so I've left the back door open. Don't close it."

"Okay. I may be gone by the time you get back. I've got a few errands to run." He kept his back to her as he took off his hat and ran his fingers through his hair.

Laurette smiled grimly to herself. Neither of them was telling the truth, but she wasn't going to press Grandfather. If he wanted to check on his still, that would give Jeff a chance to dust for fingerprints without Grandfather having to know someone had been in the house.

"I'll see you later," she said, and left for Jeff's house.

She arrived there ten minutes later and parked in front of it. He wasn't home. Neither was he at the station. After deliberating for long moments she sneaked the fingerprinting equipment and manual out of the office and headed back home, intent on taking the prints herself.

Realizing that there was someone in his department who could not be trusted, Jeff also recognized

222

he would have to conduct his investigation in secret. And he thought he knew the best place to start.

After driving out to the shack on West Lane alone, he parked the car in the weeds and made his way cautiously up to the house. Daylight was fading and soon it would be dark. Inside the front door the shadows were already thick. He snapped on his flashlight and proceeded deeper into the house. Footprints were scattered around in the thick dust on the floor, some having treaded over previous ones. He would get samples of those later. Right now, however, he proceeded over the creaking floor into the kitchen and down to the basement.

In the first room of the basement he found nothing but cobwebs and some yellowed newspapers. In a smaller room that must have been used to store home-canned fruits and vegetables, he continued the same careful exploration. This time he noticed a small piece of brown wrapping paper crumbled on the floor. He picked it up and straightened it carefully. NEW YORK METROPOLITAN MUSEUM OF ART was stenciled on it and below the lettering was a fuzzy black line. He held the flashlight closer to the paper and saw that the black mark was really a tiny row of numbers preceded by two letters.

Jeff drove straight back to his house and called the New York City police. Almost immediately he was transferred to a special art squad. The man who answered identified himself in a thick Bronx voice.

"Reggie Winter here."

"This is Jeff Murray. I'm police chief here in Locust Grove, Tennessee."

"Where?"

"Locust Grove, Tennessee. It's near the Smoky Mountains."

"Yeah. What can I do for you?" There was a decided note of disinterest in Reggie's voice.

"I'm calling to find out if the Metropolitan Museum of Art has reported anything missing recently. Probably a painting, or something that would be wrapped in brown paper."

"Why?" The voice was instantly sharp and alert.

"Because I have reason to believe a local house is being used as a drop. I found a wrapping paper there with XK7219380 stenciled on it and I thought maybe—"

"Holy cow! Read that again."

Jeff did, and followed by asking politely, "Then you do have some things missing?"

Reggie was more willing to confide in him now. "We sure as hell do. Somebody's hauling stuff out of the basement of the museum as soon as it comes in. We had a whole shipment of icons from Italy stolen a couple of months ago. And that's not the half of it. Someone's using this place like it was the public library. They're just checking things out whenever they please."

"Italy," Jeff repeated pensively. Hadn't some of those long distance calls on Laurette's phone bill been to Italy?

"Give me the name of that town you're at again. I'm going to come right down."

Good. He could use the help. "Listen, while you're

here, I want you to be undercover. Don't give out information to anyone but me. Understand?"

"Sure thing. I'll be there as soon as possible."

Jeff hung up and smiled to himself. There were still a lot of loose ends, but pieces were beginning to fall into place. He felt a surge of buoyant pleasure as he walked out the door.

Night had fallen and the little sliver of a moon gave only a faint light. But it was a nice night and he wanted to spend it with Laurette. It had been a stroke of genius to take her to Memphis. Things there had gone even better than he'd expected. And he intended to see that their relationship continued to grow.

Once inside his car, he started the engine. Even though he had been busy today he had thought of Laurette often—remembering the warmth of her bare hip against his and the way her lips swelled to a ripe fullness when he kissed her. He wanted to kiss her now, but knew that would have to wait. He had work to do.

CHAPTER FIFTEEN

Jeff knew now that the thieves were dealing in stolen artwork. Reggie, the New York art cop, had arrived in town yesterday. He was a thin man with a frill of mustache above his lip and a quiet laugh. Jeff liked him. Reggie had gone to Jeff's house last night and they had sat up very late discussing strategy. Today Reggie was having a look around town and talking to local artists to find out if any of them had been approached recently by anyone buying or selling paintings.

For his part, Jeff had begun quietly checking the backgrounds of the police officers who worked under him, looking for a clue as to who might be in league with the robbers. He was also listening to their conversation with a sharp ear on the off chance they'd accidentally reveal something.

In addition, he was trying to give the impression he'd learned a lot in Memphis on the hope the conspirator would panic and do something foolish.

He also intended to try to keep some of the men under surveillance in the evenings. That would be difficult since he'd have to do all the work himself.

But he didn't want to ask the sheriff for help, reasoning that the fewer people who knew about this investigation the better. He had been so busy planning his moves that only late last night when the crickets had hummed and the wind had stirred in the trees was he able to forget the tension of his work and let his thoughts float in a sea of memories of Laurette. The memories kept him going, but they weren't, unfortunately, as good as the real thing. He didn't know when he and Laurette would have a chance to spend time alone again; it might be a while. But he couldn't rest until he'd made an arrest on the robbery.

Jeff had virtually ignored Laurette all morning. He had been so busy, she hadn't even had a chance to tell him about the stranger in her grandfather's house or to show him the prints she'd taken from the phone and doorknob. Lifting them hadn't been difficult; she had done everything according to the instructions, and she thought she'd gotten a good set.

Sighing, she looked blankly at the computer screen. She had come to this town with no intention of staying. But that was before she'd begun to care for Jeff. She thought he cared for her, too, but somehow they didn't seem to be connecting.

When their eyes did finally meet, however, Jeff's smile was so full of tenderness that her own softened to match. But then he disappeared back into his work, and she was left feeling bereft and even more confused.

It was just before noon when he came over to talk to her. She felt her breath jam in her throat when he stopped by her desk and put his hand idly atop the computer. "You really have been keeping busy," he said with that smile she liked so well. "What are you doing?"

"Putting the list of the goods in the stolen property room onto the computer."

"Oh." His brows dipped into a troubled frown. "I'd hoped you were plotting the locations where moonshine had been found," he said. "Finding the gunmen is number one priority, but I also intend to make an arrest on whoever's running that still." His smile suddenly became more personal, excluding everyone around them. "You could be a big help to me by isolating the area where the most liquor has been found."

Laurette didn't know whether to laugh or to cry. She didn't want to get involved with this particular case. After maintaining her silence about the still for so long, it would be difficult to tell him the truth now. He'd want to know why she hadn't told him sooner. Then there was the problem of not being sure that he wouldn't arrest her grandfather.

"Will you work on that as a special favor to me?" he asked.

"Yes, I—I will. It may take me a while," she added, and launched into a convoluted explanation of possible problems. Actually, there were no problems and she could have made the plot within a half hour . . . if she'd wanted to.

"Just do the best you can," he said.

From across the room Burris yelled, "Laurette, phone call for you."

"Thanks." She picked up the extension as Jeff started to leave. It was Helga, bubbling with news.

"I've found the perfect job for you!"

"You've found a job already?" Laurette asked in a stunned voice. Jeff must have heard her, for out of the corner of her eye she saw him turn back toward her.

"In Louisville. It's in a bank and the pay is excellent! They're dying to interview you."

"Oh," was all Laurette could manage. It was happening so fast. "I—let me get back to you. I need a little time to think."

"Don't wait too long." Helga's voice was weighted with disapproval. "You might not get another offer this good."

"Yes, I'll let you know soon. Good-bye." She felt like someone who had paddled furiously to the middle of the ocean before coming to a realization of the enormity of what she'd done and doesn't know how to get back to shore. She had taken a big step toward putting Locust Grove behind her, but now she wasn't sure she wanted to.

Looking up, she saw Jeff standing beside her desk. "Have lunch with me today, Etty," he said abruptly.

She nodded. "Yes, there's something I have to talk to you about."

He looked at her questioningly. Just then Burris announced a long-distance call for Jeff. "We'll talk at lunch," he said firmly, and then walked away.

She went back to her task of putting the list of stolen property onto the computer, but her mind was elsewhere. Should she take the job? Could she be happy in Louisville or anywhere away from Jeff?

At twelve thirty he came back to her desk. "Ready?"

"Yes."

Taking her arm, he led her out the back door and toward his car.

She blinked up at him. "But I thought—"

"Let's go to my house, where we can talk in private."

Laurette sat silently as he drove to his house. Once they reached it he pulled her through the front door, wrapped his arms around her, and kissed her until her lips melted against his own. He continued to hold her tightly, as if by loosening his grip she might slip completely away from him. His kiss was both gentle and possessive. When she finally drew back she was breathless.

"Mmm, I'd forgotten how good you taste," he said approvingly, then was suddenly grave. He drew her toward the sofa and they both sat down, all the while keeping his hands locked over hers. "I couldn't help overhearing what you said on the phone. Are you going to take the job?"

"Jeff, I don't know. I—"

He stopped her with a shake of his head. "No, I shouldn't have asked that. Not before I said what I have to say. The weeks since you've been here have been the best ones of my life. I can't imagine your leaving and I don't want to. We're good together, Etty."

He released her hands, rose, and stalked around

the room. "I know this isn't the right time to talk about commitment. Those kinds of things should be brought up over a romantic dinner and moonlight, not squeezed in during a short lunch hour. But I can't be away from the office long and I can't give my full attention to work until I know that you're not going to leave."

Without giving her a chance to speak, he continued. "I know you may not be ready to think about marriage again, but at least promise you'll stay in Locust Grove. If you leave to take a job somewhere else, we'll lose what we're building and we'll never know if it could have worked between us. If it doesn't work, you could go then, but please don't leave now." He combed his fingers roughly through his hair and said hoarsely, "This is coming out all wrong."

"It sounds right to me," she said softly. Her indecision and doubt had been vanquished by his words and the simple need in his voice. Jeff wanted her to stay with him and she wanted to be with him. There seemed nothing more to add. Quietly she rose and went to him.

"Then you'll turn down the job?" he asked in a voice alternating between disbelief and hope.

Laurette nodded.

His lips tilted upward to form a budding smile. The smile became a beam of happiness, and then a chuckle. "You will?" he repeated, incredulous.

She was laughing when she nodded again. "Yes, I will."

He tangled his fingers around hers, kissed her with

quick exuberance, and hugged her so forcefully, it knocked the breath from her.

For a long moment he stood staring at her like a child who'd unexpectedly been given a bicycle for Christmas and can't quite believe it's his. Then his smile slipped from his face and he pushed his hands through his hair in agitation. "I want to be with you every minute, Etty, but that's not possible right now. You do understand, don't you?"

She bit her lip. "I'm trying to," she answered truthfully. "I want to."

"But when this case is solved, we'll have time for leisurely dinners and long walks and just being together."

She smiled. "It sounds perfect."

"It will be, Etty," he said soberly, "but that will have to wait a while, not because I care less for you than I do for my work, but I wouldn't be able to face myself if I didn't solve this case."

"I know." For the first time she felt that she really did understand.

She laid her head on his shoulder and put her arms around him. Everything was going to work out perfectly. She didn't even mind sharing him for a while with his work because she knew he would come back to her. He had promised her the future and she believed him.

He brushed aside wisps of hair dusting against her eyebrows and touched his lips to her forehead. "Do you know that I think of you every night when I'm lying in that empty bed? I wish you could be with me every night."

Her smile turned playful. "I'm afraid Grandfather would be scandalized."

Jeff laughed. "Yeah, he probably would, especially since he doesn't seem to be crazy about me anyway."

She traced the line of his cheekbone with her fingertip. "I'm crazy about you though."

"That's good enough." His lips settled on hers, dancing across them with urgent entreaty. Her own lips parted in response and his tongue moved into the warm interior of her mouth. As her eyelids fluttered closed she gave herself over to the smoldering drama of their kiss.

When he finally lifted his head she said seductively, "Did I hear you mention bed a while ago?"

Laurette could see the battle raging behind his eyes. Desire fought with duty and desire seemed to be winning. The idea of sinking down together on the bed kindled a fire that swirled through her. But another voice reminded her that this was the wrong time to give in to passion. Jeff was expected back at the office. Reluctantly she stepped away.

"What's wrong?" he asked.

"We don't have time . . ."

He silenced her with another kiss, but it was briefer and already the scent of passion was fading. "You're right," he said. "In fact, we need to be leaving now." With a hand on her shoulder they started back out to the car. "We'll have time later, Etty. All the time in the world."

She nodded contentedly. For now it was enough just to know that Jeff wanted to be with her. The loneliness that had stalked her for the past months seemed to have been wiped from her life with a single stroke. She wasn't going to be lonely from now on because Jeff was in her future. And he had made it plain that marriage was what he ultimately wanted. That idea was gaining in appeal with each passing minute.

"What was it you wanted to tell me?" he asked as he backed the sedan out of the driveway.

"What?" she asked dreamily.

"You said you had something to talk to me about," he prompted.

"Oh, yes." Yanked back into reality, she told him about yesterday's intruder and about lifting the fingerprints from the door when she hadn't been able to get in touch with him.

Jeff stopped for a light, turned slowly, and stared at her. "Someone was in your house yesterday?" he asked in a dangerously quiet voice.

"Yes." She tried to keep her voice calm, although the memory still frightened her. But Jeff was under enough pressure without worrying about her.

"And you're sure it wasn't your grandfather?"

"Yes. I think whoever it was has been making all those long distance calls," she said.

His brown eyes clouded over with worry. "I don't like this one darn bit. Maybe you should leave town for a few days."

Her eyebrows flexed upward. She might be scared, but she didn't want to leave Jeff! Not now. "We've just today agreed that I was going to stay. Besides," she added reasonably, "Grandfather would never leave town, which means he would be left at the house by himself, and if someone's tromping in and out of there, I don't want him left alone."

Jeff's frown underscored his reservations.

"This has been going on for months and no one has been hurt," Laurette pointed out. That was the one soothing thing she had been able to tell herself since she'd discovered the intruder yesterday. But she still hadn't slept well last night.

"Not yet anyway," Jeff said grimly. He pulled in behind the police station and parked the car. "I want you to swear you won't tell anyone about taking the fingerprints. If that became known, it might put you in danger."

"I won't tell a soul," she assured him.

"And be very careful when you're by yourself," he continued sternly. "And *don't* do any more amateur police work on your own."

She nodded meekly. His concern for her caressed her. "I won't."

"I'll send the prints to the lab and have them tested. Maybe we'll get lucky and find out who's at the root of all this."

"I hope so."

He got out of the car and she followed. "When will we be able to see each other?" she asked, trying not to sound plaintive.

"I don't know." He paused outside the back door and fitted his palm beneath her chin. "As soon as possible," he added, and dropped a kiss on her mouth. "Okay?"

"Okay." It wasn't the best she could hope for, but his second kiss helped soften the blow.

As she entered the office she was sure her blush of happiness must be apparent to everyone. All the obstacles that had kept her and Jeff apart had been battered down. They belonged to each other now. After all these weeks of trying to deny her feelings it felt good to let them out. She positively glowed.

Jeff went directly back to work, but Laurette found it impossible to do so. She felt far too happy to settle down and talk to a computer. She wanted to share her newfound joy with someone. Kathy would probably be home, but that would mean leaving the office . . . and Jeff. Even though he was wrapped up in his work, it was thrilling enough to be in the same room with him, and she didn't want to leave.

Although she remained at the office the rest of the day, she accomplished little. Most of the time she was gazing raptly at Jeff. His every move was a source of fascination and pride.

When he left shortly after five there no longer seemed any reason to remain. She was just picking up her purse and preparing to leave when Belinda came in.

"Hi. Where's Jeff?"

Walley mumbled some unintelligible answer while Laurette stood in silence. In the joy of the last few days, and especially this afternoon, she had forgotten about Belinda and her attraction to Jeff.

Laurette paused uncertainly. Should she tell Belinda about herself and Jeff? After all, she and Belinda were friends, and it seemed only fair to let her know the truth. However, it could also seem like gloating on Laurette's part. At any rate, she decided, it might be easier for Belinda to learn the facts from someone else.

Belinda waved to her. "Hi, Laurette. I've got to run now, but I'll call you sometime this week and we can get together for lunch."

Laurette mustered her enthusiasm. "Sounds great."

"See ya." The other woman disappeared out the door.

Laurette followed slowly. It could have been Belinda whom Jeff had fallen in love with, she reflected. After all, Belinda had been available and had made no secret of her interest in him. But it hadn't been Belinda; it had been her whom he had fallen in love with, and she felt awed and outrageously happy. She also felt a tinge of guilt at being so happy, almost as if her happiness were at Belinda's expense.

But Laurette couldn't remain pensive or depressed for long. Not today. She felt too much like skipping and singing.

She didn't lose her smile until she reached the house and bounced through the living room and into the kitchen. Grandfather was unloading a grocery bag. He didn't see her but she watched with a growing sense of outrage while he lifted five sacks of sugar from the bag. No wonder he went to Mountain View to shop; he was buying supplies for the still.

"Grandfather," she said in a low, accusing voice.

He stiffened and turned toward her.

She swept her hand over the sacks of sugar. "What is all that for?"

237

"Things," he answered with cold dignity.

She folded her arms across her chest and tapped her foot on the floor. "Grandfather, what is it going to take to make you realize how foolish this is?"

He grumbled inaudibly.

With a sigh of frustration she turned away from him. This was going to go on and on unless she told Jeff. Surely now that she and Jeff had committed themselves to each other she could tell him the truth about Grandfather.

"I'm going out for a walk," the old man announced. He left by the back door, slamming it behind him so hard it continued to reverberate with his anger over her scolding.

Laurette rested her elbows on the marble counter and cupped her chin in her palms, but she couldn't concentrate long on Grandfather. Soon her thoughts had danced back to Jeff and she felt carefree and happy again.

Jeff rubbed his hands over his eyes and took a drink of coffee. It was almost midnight and his body was tired, but his mind was too active to sleep. The report from the lab on the fingerprints Laurette had taken had come back this evening. The prints matched the unidentified set left at the police station by one of the gunmen.

That meant that whoever had left the prints must live in Locust Grove, probably near Laurette. And the person had been in her house, a fact that upset Jeff tremendously. Moodily he drained his coffee cup and settled back in a well-worn chair in the living

238

room. His timing had been completely off. Only today he had asked Laurette to stay in town, and now he wished he hadn't. He didn't want her to leave for good, but he did want her out of that house. What if the guy returned? There was no one there to defend her except her grandfather, and he was too feeble to defend even himself.

The phone shrilled and he picked it up. "Hello."

"Reggie, here," the other policeman identified himself tersely.

"What's up?"

"Sorry to call so late, but I think I may have a lead."

Jeff gripped the receiver tighter. "Who?"

"Do you know a man by the name of Avril Harrison?"

Laurette's grandfather! "Yes, yes, I know him."

"Well, I checked his bank account and he's been making some hefty deposits for a man who's on Social Security. He's also been making some long distance calls to Italy and New York."

Jeff's hand went slack around the receiver.

"Are you still there?"

"Yes, I'm here." He distractedly scraped his hands over his forehead. "Listen, I know about the calls to New York and I'm not sure the old man is making them. That might be a mix-up on the part of the phone company."

"Could be," Reggie said laconically, "but he's definitely making the deposits."

"I see." Was it possible the old man was involved in art smuggling? Jeff asked himself. Surely not, he reasoned before a more detached and analytical part of his mind assumed control. Maybe Mr. Harrison was making those long distance calls and trying to throw everyone off by insisting he wasn't. Even the unidentified fingerprints on the door took on new significance in light of these findings. The gunman who had left that print could have been visiting Avril Harrison to discuss business.

"I'll keep snooping around, but I thought you'd like to know," Reggie said.

"Yeah, I appreciate it. By the way, who put you on to Harrison?" Jeff asked.

"An old man at Cal's Pool Hall—fellow by the name of Izzy."

"Thanks a lot, Reggie. I'll talk to you tomorrow."

Jeff broke the connection and sat staring at the bare wooden floor. More than ever he wished Laurette had left town until this case was solved. From the looks of things, they could get very ugly. And his relationship with her would definitely suffer if he began investigating her grandfather.

CHAPTER SIXTEEN

At eight o'clock the next morning Laurette sat down in front of the computer and glanced toward Jeff's empty desk. Last night, after lying awake until after midnight, she had made up her mind to tell Jeff about Grandfather's still. Together she was sure they would come up with a solution.

But Jeff didn't come into the station until after ten, and when he finally arrived he looked tired and irritable. Her heart sank. Clearly this was not the right time to discuss Grandfather's illicit activities.

She turned back to the computer. In spite of Jeff's request that she plot a map showing locations where moonshine had been discovered, she continued keying in a partial list of the goods in the stolen property room. On an impulse she directed it to compare the items in the stolen property room against the unrecovered property of homeowners who'd been burglarized over the past year. The printer beside the computer screen began to whirl and click. It typed an item, moved to the next line, and typed another. Surprised, Laurette leaned forward to watch as a third item began to appear. The printer moved to the fourth line and began to print again.

"Oh, my gosh," Laurette murmured. A good many stolen articles had actually been recovered by the police but were languishing in the police's property room!

Swiveling in her chair, she called to Jeff. "Come here! I have something to show you."

He looked up with the harassed expression of an overworked man. "Can it wait because—"

"No!"

Pushing back his chair, he walked over to her. "Yeah, what is it?" he asked curtly.

She pointed to the computer screen. "See this television that was taken from the Cleerys last year?" Without waiting for his answer, she pointed to the printout and raced on excitedly. "It's across the alley. And so is the microwave and bicycles taken from the Fosters and the stereo the Manfords lost nine months ago." The printer was still clicking steadily away. "Look at that! There are dozens of things stored next door that belong to people whose houses were broken into."

Jeff sat down beside the printer and scanned the list. "My God." His jaw flexed into an unyielding line. "Wait till I get my hands on Walley." His face was white with anger.

Laurette bit her lower lip. Since Walley was in charge of stolen property, he was going to catch hell for letting this mix-up happen. She wondered if he might even lose his job. Clearly he'd been negligent, but she couldn't help feeling sympathy for him.

The printer continued merrily typing out words and Jeff glowered at it, then transferred his gaze to her. "I thought you were going to work on that plot."

"Well, I—".

His eyes bored into her.

She shifted uncomfortably. "I'll, um, get right on it."

His gaze moved to the floor and when he looked back at her there was regret in his eyes. "I'm sorry, I don't mean to be abrupt with you," he said in words so low only she could hear him. He touched her hand. "I'm afraid I'm a little on edge today."

"Anything you care to talk about?" she asked quietly.

"Maybe later." He squeezed her hand, then was gone.

Laurette looked after him, wondering at this man who could be hard as nails one minute and gentle and considerate the next.

Just then Walley came through the back door.

"I want to talk to you," Jeff said in a voice that could have cut stone.

Walley shifted uncomfortably. "Right now?"

"Yes. Out back." Jeff marched across the room. Both men stepped out into the alley and the door closed after them with an ominous thud.

Beside Laurette the printer clicked away and she looked at it with a tinge of guilt. Of course she'd had no choice except to tell Jeff what she had discovered. Neither did she deny that Walley deserved a reprimand. But she hoped Jeff wasn't too hard on him.

She'd had a soft spot for Walley since he'd gone to rescue Belinda.

"I checked those New York and Italian phone numbers," Reggie said.

"What did you find out?"

It was almost eleven P.M. and Jeff and Reggie were sitting in the empty police station with their feet on the desk and discarded cartons of Chinese food nearby.

"Just like I figured, the Italian number is the warehouse where the art is stored, under armed guard, until it's shipped. Whoever is calling that number must be finding out exactly when the works will be sent. The New York numbers are listings for several different art museums." He put his hands behind his neck and settled back in the wooden chair. "This is quite a ring they've got going. They seem to have people on the inside at all the important points and it's brilliant to move the stolen art to an area as remote as this. While we've been trying to track down the paintings in Los Angeles and San Francisco galleries they're being stored in a vacant building outside of Locust Grove, Tennessee, where no one would ever think to look."

"But how do they eventually fence the stuff?" Jeff asked.

Reggie rolled his thumb and forefinger over his mustache. "They probably sell it to private collectors who are so hot to have a Renaissance painting they don't question its origin. A lot of art collectors are like that. They just want to own a great work of art and don't care if they're the only one who ever sees it."

"Hmmm." It was difficult for Jeff to concentrate on art when his thoughts kept pivoting toward Laurette. Without his willing it, every image of her that came to mind was unbearably sensuous. He thought of her tracing the tip of her tongue across her lips, saw her skirt dancing around her legs, saw her enticing him from beneath the covers with a come-hither expression.

". . . don't you agree?" Reggie asked.

Jeff looked up blankly. "What?"

Reggie laughed and pushed his chair back. "Never mind. Why don't you go home and go to bed?"

"Sounds good." It would sound even better if Laurette could join him there.

"I'm going to keep an eye on this Harrison character." Reggie started for the door. "By the way, I know his granddaughter works here at the police station. You don't suppose she could be leaking information to him?"

"Absolutely not!"

Reggie shrugged. "You know how it is in police work—it's always the people you least suspect. And you said yourself someone in the station is part of this theft ring. Seems to me it could easily be her. I believe I'll keep an eye on her too," he concluded before the door closed behind him.

Jeff heaved a frustrated sigh. This was getting more and more complicated. He could hardly forbid Reggie to consider Laurette as a suspect just because he happened to be in love with her. But if she ever found out that she was under surveillance, he could imagine how that would color their relationship.

He wearily massaged his cramped leg. Things were getting worse and worse around here and he wished Laurette would leave town for a while. Not only was she in danger because someone was coming into her house, but she courted danger by doing amateur police work on her own—like going to that shack with Walley and then lifting those fingerprints. She'd even wanted to help find the traitor in the police department by asking his men questions. Yes, she would definitely be better off away from here for the present, but he knew she would resist any orders he gave her to that effect. Maybe the only way to handle this was to make her angry enough with him to leave on her own accord.

Walley was emptying a desk drawer into a cardboard box the next morning when Laurette arrived at work. She watched him for a moment in silence. Jeff, the only other person in the room, was absorbed in writing a report.

Taking slow, indecisive steps, she walked to Walley's side. "What are you doing?"

"I'm cleaning out my desk. Today's my last day."

"Oh?" Her eyes sought Jeff's, but he didn't look up.

"Have you quit?" she asked.

"I've been fired." Walley knelt on the floor and busied himself taking the contents out of a bottom drawer.

"Oh," she said again, and stood helplessly. "I'm—I'm sorry to hear that, Walley."

He made no reply.

This time when she looked toward Jeff their eyes did meet. Hers were full of reproof; he stared back with a cold look that warned her not to question his decision.

Color seeped into her cheeks. This was the man who had lain beside her and murmured tender words. How could he sit there looking so cool and harsh? It was as if there were two Jeff Murrays and this was one she really didn't know—and didn't much care to know.

Walley straightened and placed a few last items in the cardboard box. "I've taken everything out of my desk," he said with stiff dignity.

Although Laurette knew the announcement was made to Jeff, Walley never looked in Jeff's direction.

Jeff said nothing.

Walley hefted the box off the desk and carried it to the door. She hurried over to open it for him.

"Thanks," he said tersely.

"You're welcome. And good luck," she added feebly before closing the door behind him. She let go of the doorknob and rotated slowly to face Jeff. "What happened?" she asked in a tight voice.

"I fired him."

"I *know* that, and I know he'd been irresponsible, but did you have to be so drastic? He's not a young man, and I doubt he has much other experience. What will he do now?"

"I don't know and I don't care." With a brusque

247

rattling of papers Jeff turned back to the report on his desk.

Laurette was not going to be dismissed so quickly. "What kind of attitude is that?"

"It's the attitude of a man who has a police department to run," he growled. "And I want everyone to know that anyone who doesn't do their job is going to be out on their ear." After a moment's pause he added nonchalantly, "You don't have to worry. I'm happy with the work you're doing."

Her mouth fell open. "You're happy with the work I'm doing!" she repeated incredulously. In that single statement he seemed to have reduced her from a woman he cared about to a hired hand. "Just what is that supposed to mean?"

His brown eyes were agate-hard. "Just what I said. You're in no danger of being fired."

"I wasn't worried that I was," she flared. "It isn't my job that's under discussion, although if it were, I would expect a little more compassion than you showed Walley."

He looked back at the papers on his desk. "If you'll excuse me," he said coldly, "I have work to do."

"Oh, no, you don't. We started this conversation and we're going to finish it. *You're* the one who begged me to come to work here. Don't act as if you're doing me a favor to keep me on."

Jeff pushed his chair back and rose to his full height. He looked as grim as a gunman in a western about to go for the draw. "Don't do me any favors by staying on if you don't want to."

She folded her hands over her chest. It was an attitude that suggested defiance, but she was doing it partly to keep her hands from shaking. "Exactly what are you suggesting?"

"That you can quit if you have any problems with the way I run this place."

Laurette's agitation turned to astonishment. What was the matter with him? Not two days ago he had pleaded with her to stay in Locust Grove and had said they were going to plan their future when this case was settled. Now he seemed to have made a complete about-face.

Was it possible Jeff had been attracted to her only when she had seemed elusive to him—like a butterfly between blossoms? No, she argued silently, Jeff wasn't like that. But what was Jeff like? another voice countered. This stern, uncompromising man standing on the other side of the room seemed to bear no resemblance to the gentle lover she'd known in Memphis.

"I don't understand what's going on," she said with simple honesty. "Do you want me to leave? Is that it?"

He raked his fingers through his hair, looked from one side to the other, then sank back into his chair. "It might be better if you did." He toyed with a pen and didn't look at her.

"Better for whom?" she persisted.

"Better for you. Better for both of us," he added more forcefully. "The time isn't right for us."

"Because of this case?" she demanded. "Is that it?

You don't want me in your life now because you have far better things to occupy your time?"

He didn't reply.

"Fine!" She could feel herself losing her grip on her emotions, but she didn't care. "I don't want to clutter up your life and get in the way of your precious duty. But don't think when this is cleared up that you can just whistle and I'll come running back. It's over between us." Striding across the room, she grabbed her purse.

Her temper carried her out the door and halfway down the block. She didn't need Jeff Murray. But the fire of outrage was burning lower by the time she reached the second block and the pain of Jeff's rejection was beginning to sink in. Maybe she had been too quick to anger. He was tired and overworked and had surely said things he didn't mean. She should have been more understanding and sat down and talked reasonably with him. But she'd let hurt feelings and crumpled pride get the best of her common sense.

By the third block her steps had slowed and she was lost in introspection. No, she had not been too quick to anger, she realized as the pieces slowly fell into place. Jeff had wanted her to do exactly what she had done. He had goaded her into leaving. Why? Was it because he had come to realize he would never be able to give her the attention and affection she craved? Or did it have something to do with yesterday's suggestion that she leave town for a while?

Whatever Jeff's reason for wanting her to leave, it demolished her to know he could let go of her so easily. They had been building a sandcastle inch by inch, and he had come in like the beach bully and kicked it down. Inside her chest a hollow feeling warned of the approach of tears.

By the time she reached the porch steps her vision was already blurring and her lower lip had begun to tremble. How could Jeff be so callous toward her? Whatever his reasons might have been, the result was the same. She felt shattered and betrayed, and she couldn't forgive him for that. She meant what she had told him before she left the station. It was over between them.

Jeff sat brooding for fifteen minutes after Laurette left. A half dozen times he had reached for the phone, even started dialing, but had always put the receiver back down. He'd wanted to drive her away, and he had succeeded. Now he knew that he might have succeeded all too well and might have lost her permanently.

In one quick motion he grabbed the phone and began dialing her number. He would make it right between them again. He'd apologize and tell her he loved her and would do anything to keep her with him.

The back door opened as he finished dialing and Laurette's phone began to ring. Reggie slipped inside, slanting a look around to make sure they were alone before saying, "I think we should go to a judge and get a warrant to search Avril Harrison's house."

Laurette's phone rang a second time. Jeff stared at him. "On what basis?"

"I saw the old man going out into the hills today carrying a bulging paper sack, and when he came back he was empty-handed. I figure he met someone up there and made an exchange."

"Artwork doesn't bulge," Jeff objected.

"It does if it's a bunch of rolled up canvases."

Jeff put the phone down during the third ring and faced the depressing vision of appearing before Laurette with a warrant to search her grandfather's house. That would be putting nails in the coffin of their relationship.

"Can't we hold off on this, Reggie?" Jeff asked.

The other man threw him an exasperated look. "Why?"

Why, indeed? Because he was in love with Avril Harrison's granddaughter and this would kill any chance of getting back together? While that might be a very good reason to Jeff, he didn't think it was going to make much of an impression on a cop who'd come all the way from New York City to make this arrest.

Jeff managed to come up with an answer that seemed more persuasive. "If we search his house, that'll alarm the other members of the ring and we'll have less chance of catching them."

Reggie pondered that with a frown. "If we applied a little pressure, I'm sure we could get their names from the old man."

Great, Jeff thought despondently. Giving Laurette's grandfather the third degree wasn't going to endear him any further to her. "Let's hold off on this a little longer," he said. Reggie acknowledged the finality in his words with a brief, disgruntled nod and disappeared out the back door.

Jeff looked back at the phone, but he didn't pick it up again. What he had to say to Laurette would have to be said in person. First, however, there were other problems to be cleared up.

"You've got company," Grandfather called up the steps.

Laurette blotted the handkerchief against her eyes. "Who is it?" she asked faintly, but he must not have heard, for he didn't answer.

She brushed aside another tear and turned to look at herself in the mirror. It was not a pleasing sight. Her eyes were red-rimmed and her cheeks puffy from crying. She reached for her makeup bag, then let her hand fall back to her side. Powder wouldn't cover the anguish anyway.

With a sigh she started down the steps. Had Jeff come to see her? she wondered and felt a glimmer of hope that was quickly dampened by anger. If he had, she wouldn't talk to him. She had meant what she'd said earlier.

Although she wasn't afraid to face him, she still had to stop on the bottom step, take a deep breath, and pat her chest before she felt ready to go into the living room.

There she saw Belinda seated in a chair beside Grandfather watching television. "Hi, Laurette," she called.

"Hi." Laurette produced a wavering smile. "It's good to see you." Grandfather had the television

253

turned up loud and she had to pitch her voice higher to make herself heard. "Would you like something to drink?"

Belinda nodded. "I'll help."

Once inside the kitchen, Belinda pulled the door closed behind her. "Is something wrong?"

"No, I'm just catching a cold."

The dark-haired woman nodded and watched Laurette get two glasses from the cabinet. "I understand Walley was fired today."

"Yes." A sniffle slipped out.

Belinda took the glasses from Laurette's hand and set them on the table. "Why don't you tell me what's bothering you? And skip the song-and-dance about a cold, because I don't believe you. I know what a woman looks like who's been crying and from the looks of your face I'd say you've had a good two-hour cry."

Laurette smiled weakly. "Three hours," she corrected.

"Why?"

Laurette bit her lower lip. Belinda had been attracted to Jeff long before Laurette had ever come to this town. Maybe Jeff and Belinda could make a go of it once she was gone. Just because she was devastated, what point was there in letting Belinda know about her and Jeff? It would only hurt Belinda.

"Is it because of Jeff?" Belinda asked.

Laurette recoiled in surprise. "You—you know about that?"

The dark-haired woman's laughter filled the kitchen. "You've got to be kidding. I'm not blind. Besides, this town isn't that big. There've been lots of rumors swirling around about you two. At first I chose not to believe them, but that got pretty hard to do."

"Belinda, I—"

The reporter held up a hand in traffic-cop fashion. "Let me finish. I spent a couple of days being jealous of you and hoping your hair would fall out and you'd lose your teeth." She spread her hands in an elaborate gesture of helplessness. "But I liked you. We'd become friends, and who wants a bald-headed, toothless friend?"

Laurette chuckled. "Thanks."

"Besides, I'm almost over Jeff," Belinda said. "So tell me what the problem is."

Laurette pulled out a chair and slumped down into it. "Everything."

Belinda found tea in the refrigerator, poured them each a glass, and shoved one into Laurette's hand. "Start from the beginning."

Where had it begun? she asked herself. Had it started the first time he'd smiled at her? The first time he'd kissed her? "I intended for Locust Grove to be a way station only, but then I fell a little in love with Jeff. I thought he loved me too. Yesterday he asked me to stay." Her lower lip began to weaken and she paused a minute to regain her composure. "But today he seems to have changed his mind. When I objected to him firing Walley, he practically asked me to quit. It was as if overnight he'd decided he'd made a mistake about us."

"Hmmm."

While Belinda sipped her tea in silence Laurette

255

was too distraught to do more than turn the glass around and around.

"So what are you going to do?" Belinda finally asked.

"I'm going to leave," she said dejectedly. "I can't go through all that pain again. I went through it before and in the end things fell apart anyway."

"Maybe you're blowing things out of proportion. Jeff's been under a lot of strain lately. Even if he did imply he wanted you to leave, I doubt if he means it."

Laurette was no longer sure. They fell back into silence and when Belinda spoke again it was to ask a less personal question. "Why was Walley fired?"

Laurette was able to talk more coherently about Walley than about Jeff. "Because he'd done a terrible job. He was in charge of the stolen property room, but he'd let a bunch of stuff accumulate that should have been returned to its rightful owners. I know he's been derelict in his duty, but I still feel sorry for him. After all, the guy's in his forties and jobs aren't that plentiful. I wonder what he'll do now."

Belinda shrugged. "What are you going to do now?"

Laurette's resolve wavered for only an instant before she said, "Take the job in Louisville that I've been offered."

CHAPTER SEVENTEEN

"Leaving?" Laurette's grandfather looked up from buttering his toast. "Leaving," he repeated testily, as if the word itself were a personal affront to him. "Why?"

"Because I've been offered a job elsewhere," she said with a show of calm she was far from feeling.

"You've got a job here," he argued.

"The job in Louisville is a better one. I'll be happier there." That, she reflected with black humor, was the lie of the year. Right now she didn't think she'd ever be happy again. But at least the tears had subsided and had been replaced by a kind of dull, gnawing pain.

"I was in Louisville in 'forty-six and I couldn't see a damn thing in that town to keep me there. You won't like it," he declared unequivocally.

Rising, Laurette went to stand behind his chair and put her arms around his neck. She felt very sad and forlorn right now and in need of someone to hold on to. "I'll miss you, Grandfather. Will you miss me?"

Never one to get overly sentimental, he muttered

257

and stammered before finally saying, "You've got no business going to Louisville."

She straightened and pushed back the hair tumbling toward her eyes. "Oh, yes, I do. A lot more business than I have staying here. I'll pack today and leave early tomorrow morning." The sooner she was out of town the sooner she hoped the pain would begin to abate.

"Humph."

Laurette smiled wistfully down at him. She would miss her grandfather and she hated to leave him alone. At least her worries had been eased by the fact that the couple across the street had agreed to keep an extra close watch on the house. Of course she hadn't told Grandfather that. He would have been insulted by the idea that he couldn't take care of himself.

The problem of the still remained, but she had not been able to convince Grandfather to get rid of it in the time she'd been here, so that in itself wasn't reason to stay. And she had no other reason for staying in Locust Grove.

Circling to the other side of the table, she began putting the butter and milk away.

Her grandfather watched her for a moment, his faded blue eyes sharp. "Seeing as how you work at the police station, do you have any idea who that man is who's rattling around after me?"

Laurette glanced curiously at him. "What are you talking about?"

"Some man in a blue car has been following me for the past three or four days."

258

Her eyebrows contracted in a frown. "How do you know that?"

"Because I've been seein' him everywhere I turn up. Last night I went to Cal's and was halfway through a hand of five-card stud when he sidled into the room and got himself into a game at another table. He was real casuallike, mind you, and I thought, well, maybe it was a coincidence he'd showed up where I was." The look on Grandfather's face turned crafty. "So I decided to test him."

"What did you do?" Laurette slid down into a kitchen chair, half dreading to hear what he was going to say.

"Why, I went to the gents' room and climbed out the window—just like they do on television."

"You climbed out the rest-room window!"

He grinned proudly. "I sure did. Then I got in my car and drove home. I was no sooner in the house than this blue car parks half a block away and stays there for over an hour."

"Why, that's—that's preposterous!"

Grandfather squared his scrawny shoulders. "It's true."

"Why would anyone want to follow you?" Had it been the person who had come into the house? But why would they be following Grandfather? Suddenly another answer occurred to her. "Oh, Grandfather! I'll bet he's with the federal government. They must know about the still."

"Naw, they couldn't know about that." But even as he said the words he looked distinctly uneasy.

She jumped up and paced the room. "We've got to get rid of it immediately."

He paled. "Now, let's not be hasty—"

She whirled toward him. "We haven't *been* hasty, and look where it's gotten you. You could do time at a federal penitentiary for this. Those people don't fool around."

"Why would they arrest an old man for making a little home brew?" he said reasonably.

"Because it's illegal!"

He looked genuinely confused. "But I'm a good citizen. I've paid taxes and gone to church all my life."

"That doesn't matter."

"Of course it matters!" he blustered. "They wouldn't take a God-fearing, tax-paying citizen to jail."

Laurette sat staring at him hopelessly. Grandfather really couldn't see that what he was doing was wrong and she couldn't think of any argument that would convince him. But if the man following him was a "revenuer," then her grandfather was going to be in serious trouble. Could she leave tomorrow knowing that? But how could her staying change anything? She didn't need this extra burden on top of the heartache she was carrying. It was difficult enough to cope with getting through each day and knowing that Jeff was out of her life without having to worry that her grandfather might be carted off to jail.

"I insist you do something about that still!" she said fiercely.

He tilted his head curiously, like a cat watching a mouse who's behaving peculiarly.

With her vehement declaration hanging in the air Laurette shoved back the chair and marched out of the room and upstairs.

"I'm not going to apologize to him," she muttered to herself as she began slinging clothes into her suitcase. Without pausing in her work, she wiped away the tears brimming in her eyes. Immediately they were replaced with a fresh supply. "I'm not going to cry either," she said, but that didn't prevent the tears from sliding down her cheeks.

Her emotions were too high-pitched to accept examination, but she knew the reason for her tears had much to do with yesterday's parting with Jeff. Where had she gone wrong in trying to understand him? How could a man who had seemed so sensitive and thoughtful have acted the way Jeff had yesterday?

With little concern for what she was doing she jammed a silk nightgown into the suitcase and threw a robe in after it.

Downstairs, she heard the back door open and then close. From the window in her room she saw Grandfather going through the yard. He looked stooped and old and the fire drained out of her at the sight of him. How could she have talked to him the way she had?

Yes, she admitted he was a stubborn old man who could try the patience of a saint, but he was also her grandfather and she wouldn't hurt him for the world. Yet, judging from they way he shuffled along with his shoulders hunched forward, she had hurt him.

Throwing the blouse she held on to the bed, she flung open the door and ran down the steps after him.

Jeff nibbled at the sandwich, then tossed it back onto the bag. He didn't have any appetite today. Neither had he gotten any sleep last night and he knew nothing would change until he talked to Laurette and explained everything to her. And that was exactly what he intended to do right now.

He had just started to rise when the telephone rang.

"Reggie here. Can you talk?"

Jeff glanced around the office, trying not to let his gaze linger too long at the computer terminal and the empty chair in front of it. Stockwell was just leaving. Jeff waited until the door closed behind him. "Yeah. What's up?"

"As you know, I've been watching Harrison. Something very interesting just happened."

"What's that?"

"The old man and his granddaughter went out the back door. I was letting them get a little head start before following when I saw this guy stop beside their house, look around, then leap over the fence and go in the back door."

"Did you get a good look at him?"

"Yep. In fact, it was a fellow I had talked to. Howard Something-or-other. He's an artist," Reggie added.

"Howard?" Little Howie? It seemed impossible that he would be involved. Then it occurred to Jeff that everything fit. The fingerprints that weren't on

262

file must be Howie's. And he taught art, which fit right in with art thefts. Apparently Howie had even devised a creative way to avoid paying his phone bills.

"Where are you now?" Jeff demanded.

"I'm at a phone booth about three blocks from the house."

Jeff grabbed for his hat. "I'm on my way now. Get back there as soon as you can. I wouldn't want Laurette coming back and surprising this guy."

"Or the old man either," Reggie added.

"Yeah." But the truth was Jeff was so concerned about Laurette's safety, he hadn't even considered her grandfather. He knew that was wrong and unprofessional and that he was paid to protect everyone impartially. Right now, however, all he could think about was Laurette.

After a quick check to make sure his gun was loaded, he dashed out to his car, arriving in front of the Harrison house just as Reggie pulled up.

"Do you think he's still in there?" Reggie asked.

"Don't know."

Guns drawn, both men advanced toward the house. "You cover the back." As Reggie disappeared around the side of the house Jeff stepped to the side of the front door and pushed it open. "Police. Anyone in there?" he called.

No answer.

He entered cautiously. The living room was empty. So was the dining room and kitchen.

In the meantime Reggie had come in through the

back door. "We'd better look upstairs and in the basement too," Jeff said.

Reggie nodded.

But there was no one upstairs either. Reggie started back down but Jeff remained standing in the doorway of a tiny room with a wall that sloped in to accommodate the roof. On the bed was an open suitcase and women's clothing was scattered about. A hard knot lodged in his midsection and he looked quickly away. He joined Reggie in a fruitless search of the basement.

"Let's try Howie's house," Reggie called. "It's just down the street."

They walked the block to Howie's house. When no one answered the door they went around back to the barnlike studio, each keeping careful lookout as they walked. But the studio was empty too. After searching it they broke a window in the back of the house and climbed in. No one was in the house. A chill crept over Jeff. What if Howie had followed Laurette and the old man and was with them now? Howie had come to the station armed, so he was clearly dangerous.

Laurette stopped for breath on the side of the steep hill, pushed back a jumble of huckleberry bushes, and continued trudging up the overgrown hill after her grandfather. No wonder Grandfather had been convinced no one would find the still. It was certainly unlikely they would have in this godforsaken place.

"How much farther?" she called up to him.

"Not much," he answered.

She looked morosely down at her scratched hands. His words were small consolation, since he'd been saying that for the past twenty minutes. But it didn't really matter if she had to scale the Matterhorn, she told herself resolutely, as long as they got the still torn apart and the pieces hauled away to the dump, which was where Grandfather told her he had scavenged the equipment to start with.

His heart wasn't in demolishing such a work of love, but when she'd caught up with him in the alley and apologized for her harsh words, he'd told her he would do it for her.

The going grew sharply steeper and Laurette paused to find a spot in a ledge where she could get a foothold to pull herself up. By the time she'd negotiated that and looked up again, Grandfather was nowhere to be seen.

"Grandfather!"

"Up 'ere."

His voice was close by, but she couldn't see him. She scrambled upward, using tree roots as anchors. When she was on firm footing again, she looked around. "Where are you?"

He popped out from behind a locust tree. "There's a cave in 'ere."

She navigated the last few feet to him and bent to crawl through an opening. Once inside, she discovered that the cave was tall enough to permit her to stand. Light filtered in from several small openings overhead.

"How did you ever find this place?" Her voice echoed in the hollow chamber.

"We had a secret clubhouse 'ere when I was a boy. I ran away from home once and stayed up 'ere for a night." He laughed reminiscently. "Scariest damn night of my life."

"I'll bet," she murmured, and shivered in the dampness of the cave.

A light shafting in from a chink in the ceiling revealed the still. It was an elaborate setup of kettles and curling copper tubes. Devitalized lye and bags of sugar lay next to it.

Grandfather surveyed it with sad pride. "It's the best I've ever built."

"I'm sure it is," she agreed.

"You know, 'shinin' was a way of life up in these hills way back in Colonial times. Yes, sir, it sure was. It was hard to get sugar down out of the mountains and it didn't fetch much of a price, so the mountain folk used their sugar to make liquor. Why the Whiskey Rebellion that's written up in all the history books started when the government slapped a tax on the liquor. Mountain folks just didn't intend to pay it and they—"

Before Grandfather decided it would be totally unpatriotic to demolish the still, Laurette cut in briskly. "We'd better get busy taking this contraption apart."

Muttering under his breath, he put out the fire burning beneath a large kettle and began detaching the coiled tubing. "Damn shame."

"How far is the dump from here?"

"About a mile as the crow flies. Shouldn't take more than three or four trips."

266

Laurette repressed a groan. But as long as they got this apparatus carted off before whoever was tailing Grandfather found it, the trips would be worth it. She had toyed with the idea of leaving the still in place and hoping the authorities wouldn't find it, but there were two problems with that: one was that they might find it along with Grandfather's fingerprints, and the other was that her grandfather might be sorely tempted to resume business once things died down.

"Here. You carry this." He handed her a funnel and several jars.

It was no small task to climb the remaining distance to the top of the hill and weave through the overgrowth toward the dump. The brambles tore at her striped blouse and scratched at her jeans as she trailed after Grandfather.

His mind had turned to other matters. "I still don't know why you're fixing to leave 'ere. I thought you were sweet on that Murray boy. What happened to that?"

Laurette picked her way through a low-hanging clump of willows. Grandfather's question brought her squarely back to the subject she'd been trying so hard to avoid. "We weren't right for each other," she mumbled. To forestall further queries she said, "I'd rather not talk about it."

" 'Course we won't talk about it if you don't want to, but it seems strange you'd just all of a sudden pick up and leave. Seems like there must be a reason and I just wondered if it had anything to do with the Murray boy." Turning, he shot a piercing look at her. "You're not running away because things didn't work out between the two of you, are you?"

"Grandfather, please! I don't want to discuss it."

"I'm not forcing you to discuss it," he retorted. "I'm just pointing out it seems odd."

Laurette shifted the mason jars to a more comfortable position under her arms. She wasn't running away, she told herself. Jeff had accused her of the same thing, but he and her grandfather were both wrong. She was leaving because it was the wisest thing to do. But for all her wisdom, her chest felt constricted and tears lurked just beneath the surface.

"Hello there, folks."

Laurette jumped at the sound of a male voice behind her. For an instant she thought it was Jeff, and excitement and apprehension fluttered within. Then she turned and saw it was only Howie.

"Need some help?" he asked.

"Oh, hello, Howie. Thank heaven it's you!" At least he wouldn't ask any questions about what they were doing. He already knew about the still and had never told anyone.

He smiled slightly and nodded to her grandfather. "Want me to carry some of that?"

The old man turned some copper tubing over to him. "We're taking it to the dump," he said shortly.

Howie nodded and fell in step beside Laurette.

"How's everything going?" she asked pleasantly.

He gave her a strange look. "Why do you ask?"

Nonplussed, she searched for words. "No reason; I was just making conversation." They fell into silence and continued walking. Laurette had never seen the temperamental side of Howie, but she knew most artists had one. He seemed particularly hyper today, constantly looking over his shoulder and staring at her now and then with an expression she found disturbing. She was glad when they reached the dump.

Howard tossed the tubing onto a heap of broken glass. "Thanks, Howie," she said cheerfully. "You've been a big help." But she would be just as glad to see him go; he was getting on her nerves.

"We've got lots more stuff to carry," Grandfather interrupted. "He could give a hand with that too."

Howie was staring at her again. She felt distinctly uncomfortable, almost nervous under his hard scrutiny. "I'm sure he has other things to do," she said. "Don't you, Howie?"

"It's Howard," he said sharply.

"Yes, of course," she murmured.

"I'll help." But his offer sounded sullen.

Silently the threesome started back out into the hills again.

Jeff stood beside his patrol car and watched the dozen state policemen, the sheriff, and the deputies fan out into the hills. Everyone had his instructions to canvas a territory marked off in rough grids until Howard was found. Jeff had already warned them that he might be armed.

Reggie had remained behind at the office with the disgruntled local policemen. They clearly hadn't liked being excluded from the manhunt, but Jeff couldn't take the chance of turning loose the one

269

man who might try to get to Howard and warn him. Instead, he had relegated them all to "office coordination," but he thought some of them would never speak to him again.

Not that that was of much importance right now. The only thing that mattered was finding Laurette safe. As he started out into the rolling hills alongside the others he tried to push aside the thought that something might happen to her. It was now two in the afternoon and already she and her grandfather had been missing for two hours.

With his gun drawn he ventured into a dense thicket of laurel bushes and searched around. He was trying to act the cool professional, but his nerves were stretched taut. What if something had happened to Laurette? What if . . .

"See anything in there, Jeff?" one of the state policemen called.

He emerged from the laurel, straightening from his crouching position. "No, I—" He stopped, staring at the man beside the state trooper. "What the hell are you doing here, Walley?" he demanded brusquely.

"I've come to help in the search."

"You can just turn around and go home." Even if Walley were still with the police department, Jeff wouldn't have allowed him to join the search. He was as likely a candidate as anyone for being the home-grown traitor, and the fact that he had rushed out here made him look even more suspicious. "What are you doing here? Even if you were still with the department—which you aren't—you're a desk sergeant."

Walley eyed him coldly. "I may have gotten stuck with that job, but I'm a trained policeman and I can handle myself as well under pressure as any man here."

Jeff started to order him to leave, then stopped himself. If Walley were in league with Howard, perhaps he knew where to look and would lead Jeff to him. "All right, stay if you want to, but don't get in anyone's way." Without another word Jeff turned and continued tramping down a hill. Walley started off in a more easterly direction and Jeff began to drift after him. He wasn't going to let this guy out of his sight.

Not when there was a good chance Laurette was with Howard. From somewhere he thought he heard the sound of a woman's laughter, light and delicate and floating on the wind like a bird's song. He stopped short to listen, but it was already gone. It had been his imagination, he knew, but he felt a sense of loss when it ended.

CHAPTER EIGHTEEN

By the time they'd made another round trip to the dump, Laurette was tiring. Added to that, Howard was making her extremely edgy with his odd quizzical glances. She was feeling more and more aware of their isolation in these wooded hills and liking it less and less.

As they began the return journey from the dump to the cave she saw his hand go to his hip and linger there. It blurred into her mind that he had a gun concealed beneath his shirt. There was a definite bulge on the right side of his waist that looked ominous.

He was looking at her again and his eyes were wild, almost glazed. Suddenly Laurette knew this was no artist being temperamental; this was a man on the verge of a breakdown. Grandfather had his back to him and Howard moved toward the old man in what struck her as a menacing manner. If she'd had a moment to think, she probably would have talked herself out of what she did next. But she didn't think; she acted on instinct. Feigning a stumble, she picked up a rock and rose behind Howie to smash it over his head. He went down with an almost ballet-like gracefulness.

Grandfather turned around and saw Laurette standing over Howie, still holding the rock. He snorted in disgust. "What in Sam Hill did you go and do that for? Now we're going to have to carry the rest of this stuff by ourselves."

Laurette stared dumbly at the rock in her hand, then down at the inert form at her feet. What had she done? The rock slipped from her fingers and thudded to the ground. "I—I don't know why I hit him. He was acting so strange that I . . ." Her words trailed away to nothing. "You don't think I've hurt him badly, do you?"

Grandfather got laboriously to his knees and inspected Howie. "You put quite a lump on his head, but that's about it. He'll be all right directly. Why in the name of creation did you want to thump him over the head?"

Laurette fell to her knees beside Grandfather. "I thought he had a gun." Gingerly she combed her hands down his side. "He *did* have a gun," she cried, pushing back his shirttail and withdrawing the weapon from his waistband.

Grandfather frowned at it. "It's a thirty-eight Smith and Wesson. That ain't exactly the kind of gun you hunt squirrels with."

"No, it isn't," she said crisply, and forgot her remorse at hitting Howie over the head. "Come on, let's get out of here before he comes to."

Grandfather took the gun from her and turned it

273

over curiously. "Nice gun." Pointing it upward, he peered through the sights, then squeezed the trigger.

Laurette jumped. "Grandfather!"

He shot again. "Nice firing action too," he commented to himself.

The last two hours had been a strain for Laurette. Her nerves had been stretched from being with Howard and it had been an added jolt to find herself actually knocking a man unconscious. The discovery that Howard was armed and might have meant them harm was only now sinking in fully. Her knees began to turn to jelly.

"Forget the gun!" she said wildly. "Let's get out of here."

Grandfather didn't budge. "What about the still?"

She was almost beside herself. "That doesn't matter now! Don't you see, we've got to get back to town and let the police know about Howard." It was all clicking into place. Howard was the man Jeff was looking for. Howard was the man who had been coming into their house.

Grandfather began to walk beside her, complaining as he went. "Seems like you could make up your mind about what you want. This morning gettin' rid of that still was awful all-fired important and now you say forget it."

She paid no attention to him. "Maybe we should have tied Howard up," she fretted, but she knew she didn't have the nerve to go back to do that. She had to get to town as quickly as possible. "Please hurry."

He glared at her. "I'm going as fast as I can, young lady. Go on ahead if you want to."

"No." She didn't want to leave Grandfather alone and she didn't want to be alone herself. What she really longed for was to rush into a pair of strong arms and let someone capable handle this. Jeff's name came immediately to mind, and she longed for his broad shoulder and the comforting strokes of his hands through her hair.

The sound of a gunshot pierced Jeff like an arrow. The second one was even more shattering. Two shots. Had two people been shot?

The other officers were scattered across the hills and valleys around him. They, like him, paused for a moment, then began to run in the direction the shots had come from. Jeff stood another second immobilized, the weight on his feet attached directly to his heart. What if Laurette were . . .

Then he began to run with a fleetness he hadn't known he possessed, scrambling over the exposed rock on the face of a steep hill and sliding down the grassy back side.

He heard voices and shouts around him, but he didn't pay any attention to them. He'd lost track of the others, lost track of Walley, lost track of everything but the need to get to Laurette.

He raced out of a shadowed valley and into the sunlight of a broad field. Other men were already there, looking down at something on the ground. Breathlessly Jeff reached them and pushed his way through to the front. Howard lay on the ground, blinking warily up at the officers.

Jeff wanted to strangle him. "Where is Laurette?"

275

Howard rubbed his head gingerly. "I have no idea. She must have knocked me out and taken off."

He began to breathe a little easier. "Who fired those shots?"

"It sure wasn't me," Howard said, and then winced at the pain in his head.

"See to him," Jeff directed two of the men. "The rest of you can start back toward town. Keep an eye out for a woman and an old man."

He whirled and began making his way back to town, scanning the hillsides as he went. He hadn't gone far before he reached a summit and looked down onto the broad, vast valley below. Moving up the next slope were two antlike people.

Shouting as he ran, he sped down into the valley. He saw Laurette turn, then began to run toward him. They collided in the middle of the valley and he swooped her off her feet and swung her around. Her clothes were streaked with dirt and grass stains and her hair was a wispy jumble. He'd never seen anyone who looked as good as she did.

She kept trying to explain something in a breathless rush, but it didn't come out very coherently. "Jeff, you won't believe this. . . . Howie was acting so strange. . . . I mean, I didn't know that I was going to hit him but—"

He smothered her in kisses and squeezed her to him as hard as he could.

"But Howie—" she protested.

"It's all right. We've already found him and he's being taken care of." His eyes wafted over her, taking in the alluring body and then coming back to settle on her glowing face. "Have I told you that I love you?"

"No," she whispered, "but I'm willing to spend the rest of my life listening to you say it."

A half hour later Laurette was sitting at her old desk in front of the computer. Jeff had brought her to the station and left her there, promising to be back soon. Burris and Stockwell were scrutinizing her as if she were a germ on a slide, and the other men were whispering among themselves, glancing frequently toward her and her grandfather.

The door opened and a state trooper sauntered in. He moved across the room to stand beside Stockwell. "You'd better come with me."

Fear and rebellion crossed Stockwell's face. For a minute Laurette thought he was going to fight, then his shoulders sagged and he followed the trooper out the back door. So it had been Stockwell, she thought, but that didn't really matter to her right now. The butterflies she felt in her stomach weren't caused by any crime, not even her grandfather's crime; they owed their existence to her turbulent feelings for Jeff.

Now that she realized that love could heal as well as hurt she wanted to mold her future to Jeff's.

The man with the New York accent they called Reggie began taking a statement from her grandfather, who was waxing eloquent. "I knew from the minute we saw that boy up there that something was wrong. Yes sir, he just didn't act right. I suspected he had a gun on him." Grandfather nodded decisively. "Yep, I sure did."

277

Laurette smiled to herself. All around her, conversation swirled and phone calls were made. Men marched in and out of the office. She heard everything as if it were coming from a great distance away. All that was happening outside her. But only the sight of Jeff mattered to her and she looked up hopefully each time the door opened. Each time she was disappointed.

Belinda appeared a short while later and plopped down beside Laurette. "Well, this has become one heck of an exciting town."

"Do you know where Jeff is?"

"Out at the shack on West Lane. Turns out there's a hidden tunnel that goes out of the root cellar behind the house and connects to a cave. They're finding a treasure-trove of artworks in the cave. Howard and Stockwell must have masterminded the plan. Apparently Howard had enough contacts in the art world that the final list of who's involved is going to read like a phone directory.

"Howard was one of the men who broke into the police station," Belinda continued. "Apparently they had some paintings stored out there right under everyone's noses. When Howard found out Walley was going through the property room, he panicked. He had to get the stuff out of there and out to the shack. Besides, it was a good ploy to tie up Stockwell because that made him look like an innocent victim. Anyway, Jeff's out at the shack now," she concluded.

Laurette nodded. She wanted him to be with her, but she understood that he couldn't be. It didn't really matter as long as he was safe. They'd have time later.

Belinda lowered her voice and scanned the room. "Walley's out there too. He's the one who found the hidden tunnel. I guess he got to thinking how suspicious it was about that man disappearing into thin air that time I went to the house. After he got fired he had plenty of time, so he combed over the house and found the tunnel. It seems Walley was such a sloppy desk sergeant because he never wanted the job in the first place. He wanted a job with action, but the old chief chained him to a desk. Then they brought you in and he thought he was going to be replaced by a computer and lose the one little niche he had left in police work. Poor guy.

"I'm sure Walley will get his job back," Belinda continued, and patted Laurette's hand.

"I have a hunch everything's going to be fine. I've got to get over to the office and start typing. This story may even shove the annual craft show right off the front page!"

Belinda disappeared. When the back door opened a minute later Laurette's eyes darted toward it. Jeff stepped in and his eyes swept the room like a man desperately searching for something he'd lost. His gaze settled on Laurette. His mouth was a straight line, but there was a softness in his eyes that beckoned her. Oblivious to the rest of the people in the room, she stood and crossed over to him.

He touched her face as if to assure himself that she was a flesh-and-blood woman and not an illusion. Then he cupped his arm around her and drew her outside. He kissed her as if he meant to absorb the essence of her soul through their kiss. She responded with breathless wonder.

This was better than what they had shared their first night together, even better than what they had known in Memphis. This was pure, undiluted love, the kind that allows no reservations or hedging. His tongue flitted past her lips and coaxed a soft moan from her. She fitted her hands more fully around his neck and gave herself over to the sweet glory of their embrace.

Finally he drew back and whispered against her ear. "I was sick with worry about you today. From now on I'm going to keep you in my sight twenty-four hours a day."

She nodded as his mouth returned to hers. It sounded like a good plan, she reflected as she felt desire budding in his body. She knew the only way they could express the true depth of their emotions was to be as physically and emotionally close as possible.

"Jeff, let's go to your house," she whispered.

He laughed huskily. "I thought you'd never ask. What about your grandfather? Should I have someone take him home now?"

She shook her head and grinned. "No, he's in his element telling how he solved this caper. There's no harm in him hanging around and being heroic, is there?"

"No."

She glanced back over her shoulder, thinking of the bustle in the station. "Can you leave now?"

"I sure can. The important part of this case is solved. The rest of the work will be here when I get back. Your work will be here too."

A smile began to dawn, then folded. Her work. That meant continuing to plot locations to find Grandfather's still. She had to tell Jeff. Later. She would tell him later.

But he had already seen her troubled expression. "What's wrong?"

"It's—nothing."

He would not be put off. "Something's wrong."

Nodding, she fixed her gaze on his shoes. "Yes." She tried to ease into her story. "If someone were making moonshine, perhaps an older person, and they decided to quit and even began taking their still apart, well—" She paused to search for words.

A variety of emotions flitted through his eyes, ranging from incomprehension to surprise to displeasure. But the final emotion was one she couldn't read.

She pushed on. "What I'm trying to explain is—"

He held up a hand to stop her. "Etty, unless I have some hard evidence—say a still that's in place—I can't make any accusations or arrests. So I think you'd better just forget whatever rumors you might have heard."

She stared at him in confusion. And then she realized that he understood. "You mean you're going to make an exception for my grandfather?" she asked softly.

His lips crooked into a smile. "Let's just say I'm going to trade even. He helped us catch Howard, so I'm willing to do him a favor in return."

"Thank you." The simple words didn't do justice to the vast relief she felt. It was as if a weight had been lifted from her shoulders.

"I can't say that I'm thrilled you kept this from me, but I'm in a forgiving mood right now." He scooped her into his arms and crushed a kiss on her lips. Finally he pulled back. "We'd better get over to the house before I forget myself."

"Yes, we'd better." She practically purred with contentment.

Laurette snuggled up next to him in the car, wanting to be as close to him as possible. She couldn't keep her hands from wandering over his shirtfront, as if only by touching him could she reassure herself he was real and he was hers. He alternated between looking at the road and looking at her with a smile of such enormous love that she felt herself go weak.

The trip to his house seemed to take forever. Finally they were there and she was standing inside the bare little living room. It seemed like coming home.

He held her against him. "I was so worried, Etty. You can't imagine."

She nodded and felt the cotton of his shirt scratching against her cheek. "Oh, yes, I can. I know what it's like to almost lose someone you love." She had almost lost him.

He cupped his fingers beneath her chin and lifted her face to his. His mouth descended to hers with the intensity of a man too long denied. He branded hot kisses on her lips before parting them with the tip of his tongue. She tasted the stark need in his kisses and responded with a fierce desire to satisfy him in every way. Already she could feel his body throbbing to life in a display of masculine urgency.

He swept her up into his arms as easily as if she were a child and carried her toward the bedroom. Hungry for his kisses, she lifted her mouth to his and teased at the sensuous bow of his upper lip until he returned her kiss. Soon she was lying on the bed and he was sitting on the edge of it, taking off his shoes.

Although she knew he would be joining her in a moment, that didn't seem soon enough. She got up on her knees and fitted herself against the strong lines of his back, tilting her head around to catch his mouth again and resume their torrid kiss. She felt him start to hold her away, then he groaned and dragged her onto his lap, deepening their kiss until her lips were on fire.

His strong hands chased over her cotton blouse in search of buttons. In his haste he tore off two of them. She continued to cling to him, drawing fulfillment from the kisses that fused them together. Her hands were linked around his neck as if it provided a lifeline. Only when she felt his big, warm hands sliding beneath the blouse to touch her breasts did she loosen her hold and let her own hands wander.

As they grazed over his cheeks she felt the flush of desire on them and felt his body tense when her fingertips circled around his earlobe. Effortlessly he rolled her onto the bed and whisked her slacks off. Before she would have thought it possible, he had eliminated all barriers and joined their bodies together.

She expelled a cry of pleasure.

His mouth strayed over her heaving breasts, lingered on her bare shoulders, and returned to recapture her lips. She gathered him as close to her as she could, wanting to possess every inch of his hard body. All the while he continued to flex against her, causing a tight series of reactions to uncoil, beginning with a tingling pleasure in her fingertips that spread down her arms like flowing lava. Finally she felt as if her whole body was being catapulted into a realm of pleasure so deep that she began to feel weak with euphoria.

"Thank you," she murmured breathlessly.

"You're incredible" was his husky reply.

He stretched out on the bed beside her and she curled her arm around him. He was breathing quickly, as if he, too, were still partly caught in the throes of their lovemaking. She smiled. Neither of them felt like talking right now. No words could adequately express what they were feeling. Instead, she continued to hold him and felt wealthy beyond measure because he was hers.

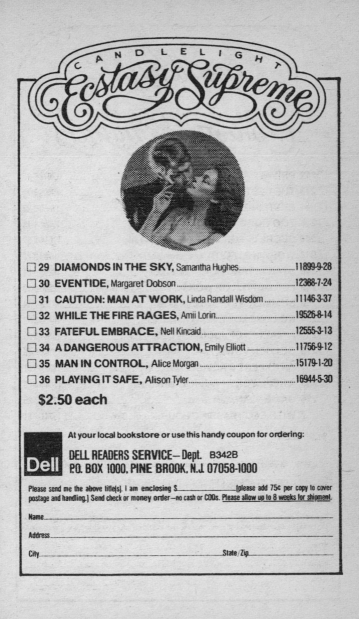

Candlelight Ecstasy Romances™

$1.95 each